A POCKETFUL OF
CROWS

Also by Joanne M. Harris from Gollancz:

Runemarks
Runelight
The Gospel of Loki

A POCKETFUL OF CROWS

Joanne M. Harris

GOLLANCZ

LONDON

First published in Great Britain in 2017 by Gollancz
an imprint of the Orion Publishing Group Ltd
Carmelite House, 50 Victoria Embankment
London EC4Y 0DZ

An Hachette UK Company

5 7 9 10 8 6 4

A CIP catalogue record for this book is
available from the British Library.

ISBN 978 1 473 22218 2

Typeset by Input Data Services Ltd, Somerset

Printed in Great Britain by Clays Ltd, Elcograf S.p.A.

www.joanne-harris.co.uk
www.orionbooks.co.uk
www.gollancz.co.uk

May Eve

✝

I am as brown as brown can be,
And my eyes as black as sloe;
I am as brisk as brisk can be,
And wild as forest doe.

The Child Ballads, 295

One

The year it turns, and turns, and turns. Winter to summer, darkness to light, turning the world like wood on a lathe, shaping the months and the seasons. Tonight is May Eve, and the moon is full for the second time this month. May Eve, and a blue milk moon. Time for a witch to go travelling.

Tonight I am a vixen. I could have been an owl, or a hare, or a lark, or a wolf, or an otter. The travelling folk can take any guise. But tonight – this special night, when wildfires burn and witches fly – tonight, I am a vixen.

I leave my clothes by the fireside. The feather skirt, the wolfskin cloak, the necklaces of polished stones. Naked, I turn in the firelight; moon-silver, fire-golden. And now I can hear the sounds of the night: the lapping at the water's edge; the squeak of a mouse in the

3

long grass; the calling of owls in the branches. I can hear the tick-tick-ticking of a death-watch beetle in a beam over half a mile away; I can catch the sleepy scent of lilacs on the common. I cast my gaze further. The vixen is near. Half-asleep in her warm earth, she senses my presence and pricks up her ears. The three fat cubs beside her are sleepy, filled with warm milk. But the vixen is restless, sensing me so close, so unfamiliar.

I send her the small, persistent desire for a run beneath the stars. She lifts her head and flexes her jaws, wary but still curious. I send her the feel of the cool night air, the mossy ground beneath my feet, the hunger in my belly. Shivering, I turn from the fire and walk into the forest. The ground is soft and damp and cold. It smells of rain, and bluebells. My skin is striped with moonlight, brown and silver under the trees. For a moment I see the vixen, red as embers under smoke, a single flash of white at her throat, trotting alongside me.

The scents of the forest intensify, a tapestry of shining threads that run in every direction. The vixen's fur is warm and thick; I am no longer shivering. For a time I run alongside her, feeling her strength and the fierce joy of hunting under a blue milk moon, with the promise of blood in the air and summer no more than a heartbeat away. Then, in a moment, we are one.

4

Wild creatures feel hunger differently. My own is deep as wintertime; frugal as old age. The vixen's is joyous; exuberant; sniffing for frogs under the turf; snapping at moths in the shining air. We reach the river – voles and rats – but I am hungry for something more. I follow the river until it leads to a place of open fields, and from there to the edge of a village, where the scent of prey is strong. I follow the trail of a speckled hen into a wooden henhouse, and there I am without mercy, leaving nothing but feathers.

The moon is ringed with silver – a sign. The air is sweet as summertime. Belly full and with blood on my jaws, I linger in the meadow mist, under the bank of hawthorn that marks the village boundary. Then after

5

a time, smelling smoke, I leave the vixen to return to her cubs and, naked in my own skin, I lie down in the sedge-grass and listen to the sounds of the night, and hear the owls a-calling, and watch the long, slow dance of the stars.

Tonight marks the coming of summertime. Fourteen summers I have known. Wildfire, hearth fire, bonfires lit against the dark. Cherry blossom, love charms, village girls with warm hearts, dancing in the circle of stones that stands around the fairy tree. The village girls are white and soft. Their laughter sounds like tame birds. Geese, perhaps, their wings clipped, plump, well fed, obedient. Village girls are new-baked bread. Village girls have blossom skin. Village girls have braided hair that shines like evening sunlight.

I am not a village girl. I am brown, and brisk, and wild. I hunt with the owl, and dance with the hare, and swim with the trout and the otter. I never go into the village, except as a vixen or a rat. The village is dangerous to our kind. The Folk would kill us if they could. But tonight is different. The hunt has made my blood sing. And so I linger under the thorn, smelling the scent of the young grass and listening to the distant sound of voices from the clearing.

There comes the sound of footsteps on the path by the hawthorn. A village girl with primrose hair is

6

standing by the fairy tree. The Folk call it that, even though they know nothing of the Faërie. But there *are* charms – the bone of a hare; a name, stitched on red flannel – that even a village girl can use. And on May Eve, by a blue moon, a love charm hung from a fairy tree may bring even a village girl the quickening of summertime.

The fairy tree is a hawthorn. Twisted and raddled, old as Old Age, half-eaten with mistletoe, she stands inside the circle of stones that some Folk call the fairy ring. Every year, I tell myself: maybe this is the year she will die. But every year the pale buds break from those cracked and knotted boughs. The fairy tree is hopeful. Her blossom barely lasts a week. But every year she quickens, and bears a handful of scarlet berries.

The girl has a charm. They always do. A love charm, or perhaps a spell to make herself more beautiful. I watch from the hedge as she ties it in place. The shadows of the fairy stones flicker in the moonlight.

Tonight she will dream of her young man, restless on her virgin's bed. Perhaps she will watch the bright May moon slicing past her window. And tomorrow, or the next day, he will see her standing there – a girl he has seen many times before, but never noticed until now – and he will wonder how he could have been so blind as to miss her.

When she has gone, I take the charm. She will think the fairies have taken it. A scrap of red fabric, the colour of blood, torn, perhaps, from a petticoat, and pushed through a polished adder-stone. I had such a charm-stone once, but I lost it long ago. Where did the village girl find hers? How long did she take to embroider the charm, by the light of her candle? What name did she speak as she knotted the thread?

I look at the tiny stitches. Six little letters, embroidered in silk. I myself cannot read words. There was no one to teach me. But I do know *letters*; those magical signs that speak from the page, or even the grave. There is power in them, a power that even the Folk do not understand. Letters have meaning. They can make words. And words can build almost anything – a law, a chronicle, a lie.

The name in the letters is W-I-L-L-A-M. This is the name his mother gave him. This is the name his lover will speak into his ear, in the dark. This is the name they will carve on his stone, when they put him into the ground.

I have no name. The travelling folk have neither name nor master. When I die, no stone will be laid. No flowers will be scattered. When I die, I will become a thousand creatures: beetles, worms. And so I shall travel on, for ever, till the End of the Worlds. This is the fate of the travelling folk. We would not have it otherwise.

I carry the charm to my place in the woods. A hut of split logs and willow and moss, all lined with skins and bracken. My firepit is just outside, and my iron cooking pot. Hungry, I fry some fiddleheads, and with them some bacon, a handful of herbs and the hindquarters of a rabbit that was hanging in the smoke. And then I tie the village girl's charm over the entrance to my hut, with all my beautiful coloured things. A blue glass bead, some yellow wool, the whitened skull of a magpie. The coloured things that I collect and hide away in the forest.

Coloured things are forbidden to us, we the canny travelling folk. Colours mean danger to our kind; they reveal us to the enemy. Our folk hide from everyone – even from each other. Our folk know to keep aloof, to never show their colours.

Village girls wear coloured things. Ribbons on their bonnets. Scarlet flannel petticoats. Village girls are not afraid. Village girls like to be noticed. But brown is easy; brown is safe. In the forest, no one sees a brown girl slip from tree to tree, to vanish in the bracken. In the forest I am a doe, a stoat, a fox, a nightingale. Berry-brown, I live in the trees. Brown, I cast no shadow.

This is how I go unseen, untroubled by the village folk. Only their dogs know where I am, and they have learnt to keep away. I have eaten dog before, and will again, I tell them. I sit on my wolfskin blanket, wrapped in my skirt of homespun cloth and my coat of sparrow feathers and I look into the smoke to see what the future will bring me.

Tomorrow is May Day. The flowery month: the month of hawthorn and of bees. Tomorrow, there will be merriment, and dancing on the village green. Tomorrow, the village girls will dress the springs and wells with flowers, and leave offerings for Jack-in-the-Green, and crown a maiden Queen of the May. But that's no concern of mine. I have no need of garlands. I have the bluebells in the wood, and the hawthorn in the hedge. No young man will steal my heart with words of love and garlands. No young man will catch my eye. When the heat is on me, I will go into a doe, and take my pick of the young bucks, and never once look back.

The vixen sleeps in the warm earth, surrounded by small, furry bodies. The brown hare in the moonlight dances on the hillside. The barn owl hunts: the field mouse runs; the fire dies down to embers. And I will go into my hut and draw the deerskin curtain, and go to sleep on my narrow bed of brown wool and of bracken.

May

The Month of Bees

†

When the ragweed blooms in May
Witches ride, and good Folk pray.

Cornish proverb

One

Today, I will be a skylark, flying sweetly into the blue. Or perhaps I shall go into a hare, and run across the hillside, and box the shadows of the sedge, and nibble at the cowslips. Today, I am restless, uncertain of what I want and where to go. Over my breakfast of broken bones, I feel the morning sun on my face and long for the freedom of the hills.

But food is not yet plentiful, and travelling must be paid for. Last night's adventure has left me weak, in spite of the strength of the village girl's charm, and so I take my collecting bag – the charm safe in my pocket – and set off for the riverside, the open fields and my willow traps, which might catch me a bird or two, or maybe even a rabbit.

Today I am lucky. I bag four thrush, some May

buds and a pocketful of fiddleheads, those tight little ferns, which, like the Folk, are so tender while they're young, but bitter poison when they grow. It is enough. I turn to go back, but suddenly I hear horses' hooves on the path behind me. A riding-horse with iron shoes, trotting at a lively pace some quarter of a mile away. Quickly, I step off the path and hide behind a deadfall of broken trees. The horseman will be gone soon, and then I will be on my way.

A few minutes later, I see the horse, a chestnut with a black mane, and riding, a man in a May-green coat, wearing a garland of flowers. Quickly, my hand seeks the village girl's charm. An adder-stone gives protection for those who do not want to be seen. The stone is smooth and cool in my hand. The scrap of scarlet petticoat shows bright between my fingers.

I would not normally look up. I do not want to be noticed. And yet I am curious to see more of the horse and its rider. Carefully, I peer out from between the spurs of the deadfall just as he passes beside me, the buttons on his green coat flashing in the sun.

A nobleman, then – I can tell by his boots, and by the way he looks around as if he owns the trees themselves. His hair is as smooth as his horse's flank. Why do I even notice him? Is it the adder-stone in my hand, that wants me to see him more clearly? I raise the polished stone to my eye and look at the man through the narrow bore. Somehow I know that he will look back. I know that his name is W-I-L-L-A-M. And now, as he turns, as I knew he would, I see that he is handsome.

Just at that moment, the fine brown horse stumbles on the stony path. The young man, taken off balance, slips and falls out of his saddle. The horse rears up, its eyes wild, its hooves striking sparks against the stones. The young man will be trampled, and there is no one to help him. And so I jump out from my hiding place and catch the horse's bridle.

A soothing cantrip: the horse is soon calmed. Wild horses are different. Wild horses do not welcome our touch. But this one is a riding-horse; nervous, but trained to the bridle. I turn now to the master, who is lying on the path. He is a little dazed by the fall, but he is out of danger. I notice that he is very young, barely older than I am. I tether the horse to a nearby branch and prepare to vanish into the woods.

'Wait.' I turn, and see him watching. His eyes are blue as a jay's wing. 'Who are you?'

I do not answer. A named thing is a tamed thing, and my people are wild for ever. I ought to ignore him and walk away. His kind are so often dangerous. And yet, he looks harmless enough on the ground, mud on the sleeve of his fine green coat, his cheek scratched by a bramble. And he sees me – really *sees* me. I can see a tiny reflection of myself in his eyes. Perhaps that's why I want to stay, to hear the sound of his voice again, to have him look at me that way and see myself in his blue eyes. No one sees me, as a rule. Even when I show myself, no one *really* sees me.

'Who are you?' he says again. His voice is as soft as deer velvet.

I shake my head.

'Don't be afraid. Who are you? Where are your people?'

My people are the wolves, the hare, the wild bees in the forest. My people are the birch trees, the roe deer, and the otter. My people are the travelling folk that travel on the campfire smoke, and go into the fox, the wolf, the badger and the weasel. And I am not afraid.

I lift my chin and say: 'The woods.'

'Then you must be the Queen of the May,' he says, and stands, and picks up his May Day garland, which has fallen to the ground. It is a garland of strawberry leaves, woven together with wild rose.

He places it gently onto my hair. 'Do you have a name?' he says.

Of course not. Names are for tame folk. Names are for those who are afraid of our kind of freedom.

I think of the village girl's adder-stone charm. I say: 'I know *yours*. It's W-I-L-L-A-M.' He smiles. I wonder why he is not surprised that I know his name. Then I realise that he knows *all* the village girls know his name. All the village girls notice him. All the village girls dream of him, and whisper his name into their pillows. The surprise would be if I did not.

For a moment his arrogance leaves me mute. But even that has a kind of charm. He reminds me of a young stag showing off his first pair of antlers. He has the same kind of awkwardness, of playfulness, of confidence. Something unlike the rest of his kind. Something almost wild.

'It's *Will-i-am*.' He writes it in the dust of the path.

W-I-L-L-I-A-M. With that extra stroke. The village girl must have spelt it wrong.

'Will-i-am.' It sounds as sweet as water from the well. He smiles again. I rarely smile. I have no one to smile for. And now I know why I took the charm from the fairy tree last night. Now I begin to understand my restlessness, my hunger. Something was missing from my life. Something I never suspected was wrong. And now, today, something has come to answer the quickening call of the May.

W-I-L-L-A-M.

W-I-L-L-*I*-AM.

It is only one letter. A single stroke. But I can feel it, nevertheless. He too has a space inside, like the hole in the adder-stone. An emptiness waiting to be filled. Something that was missing. And although I can barely read his name scratched into the dusty path, I already know in my secret heart that the thing that was missing was *I*.

TWO

Today, I am a hawthorn tree, all trembling and shaken. I slept with his garland at my side, and this morning it was still green, although the roses had faded. And so I went into a bird – a linnet, brown and busy – and sang, and flew, and flew, and sang, and yet could not leave the young man behind or forget him, as I could forget those tame young men from the village.

What sickness is this? Why do I not take pleasure in my freedom? The air is bright; the sky is blue; the wind is filled with promise. Why then do I feel so unlike myself, so restless and strange, so incomplete? Why then do I ache, and fret, and pine, and rage, and question?

I fled when, for the second time, the young man asked to know my name. He tried to follow, but was too slow and clumsy in the undergrowth. I fled through thicket and bramble and thorn, then crossed where the river ran shallowest, following the secret paths that only deer and foxes know. But *W-I-L-L-I-A-M* stayed with me somehow, and in the song of the linnet I heard his name, and in the sound of the wind, and all day from the sky I watched for his horse, and for the green of his coat, and listened for the sound of his voice. But I did not see or hear him again, and finally, I went back to my hut and tried to eat, but could not; and tried to sleep, but could not; and tried to forget him, and could not. Instead I remembered a song of the Folk; a song that maidens sometimes sing:

I took this fair maid by the lily-white hand
On a green mossy bank we sat down;
I gave her a kiss on her sweet rosy lips,
A tree spread its branches around . . .

The very next morning I made her my bride,
Just after the breaking of day;
The bells they did ring, and the birds they did sing,
And I crowned her the Queen of the May.

What witchcraft is this? What malady? I try to purge myself of him with wormwood and valerian. I am no village maiden, to sigh over bells and songbirds. I am no girl of the Folk, to dream of weddings and garlands. I should not have taken the village girl's charm from the branch of the hawthorn tree. The hawthorn is vengeful and cunning and old – to steal from her was a mistake. I pull the piece of scarlet silk from the heart of the adder-stone and throw it onto my cooking fire. The stone I drop into the stream, to tumble back towards the sea. The hawthorn will forget, in time, and things will be as they once were. And yet, for all that, *William* remains in me, like a splinter in my heart. And when I sleep at last, I dream of a night in midsummer; and in my dream he is warm and sweet, and tastes of blood and strawberries.

Three

Today I am a speckled frog in the rushes by a lake. The lake is deep and black as bog: its waters cold from the mountains. A dozen waterfalls and streams come to plunge their feet in the lake: otters live on the islands that rise above the surface. Today it is raining; soft fine rain like stitches of the finest silk. And yet there is no joy to be had, not in the lake or in the woods, not in the rain or in the open sky, for my love is far away and there is no pleasure without him.

His name is William MacCormac. I heard it from a white-headed crow, who heard it from a black sheep, who heard it from a tabby cat that lives in a dry-moated castle. The castle belongs to a rich old man called Sir James MacCormac. He is the laird of this piece of earth, and William is his only son.

A POCKETFUL OF CROWS

The travelling folk have no castles, no wealth. We do not hold lands or territories. Instead we have the mountains, the sea, the lakes and the moors and the rivers. *This* is our inheritance. But William will one day inherit everything his father owns: the castle, the horses, the farms, the sheep, the gold, the grain, the granaries. All the tame things his father owns will pass into his service. By the reckoning of the Folk, William will be a rich man. And rich men are courted wherever they go, by noblewomen and village girls; by commoners and courtesans. One day he will fall in love, and that girl he will marry. And their names will be spoken aloud in the church, and wedded to one another. And she will wear a muslin veil, and he will wear a garland. And he will give her a golden ring, to bind her to him for ever. And he will never once be mine, or look at me with love in his eyes, for who could love a brown girl who never stays in her own skin?

I wish I had kept the adder-stone. Such a stone is a powerful charm, and looking through the hole in its heart by the light of a tallow candle, you can see as far as the ocean – even, perhaps, through castle walls. If I had kept the adder-stone I would watch him as he slept. I would watch wherever he went, until at last I tired of the game. But the charm is lost, though the spell stands strong, and all I can do is hope to forget the young man in the May-green coat, who crowned me with wild roses . . .

Four

Today I am a nightingale at your bedroom window. My song is sweeter than honey, and yet you do not hear me. Instead, you sit in your chamber and read from a book bound in red leather, and sometimes you sigh and look outside, but you cannot see me, nor do you know how eagerly I watch you from my stony perch.

There is a sprig of whitethorn lying by your bedside. *Ill luck to the sleeper who lies by the may.* Tonight I shall go into a mouse, or a rat, or a housecat, and steal into your bedroom. There I shall take the bad-luck bloom and leave a wild rose in its place – a wild rose, like the ones you placed in my hair. A wild pink rose, still fresh with the dew, and tender as the morning. And then, maybe, you will think of me, and know that I still think of you.

A cat yowls in the darkness. I would not choose to travel with her. Housecats are at best only half-wild; fawning and purring for favours. But no one questions a housecat, or hinders her coming and going. Why do you sigh, sweet William? Why are you so restless? I scratch at your door: you let me in. I caper and purr at the touch of your hand.

'Puss, puss,' you say. It is almost a name. What a strange thing it must be, to be named. What a strange and terrible thing. No man will ever name me, not as a cat, and not as myself. And William is drawn to wild things, or he would never have looked at me.

'Puss, puss.' I take a giant leap onto the silken coverlet. Your bed is as big as my cabin, all drawn with curtains of heavy brocade. My claws are sheathed in gold and silk. There is a good fire in the hearth. My fur is alight with fireflies.

Are you lonely, William? Let me sleep beside you. I will be your companion tonight. I will guard your slumbers. No mouse or rat will dare to show its whiskers at your threshold. I shall sleep on your pillow, and purr, until you are mine for ever.

So *this* is what it must feel like. To be a named thing; a tamed thing; a pet. Of course it is foolish and absurd, and yet it feels good to be here at your side, your hand moving gently against my fur. Just for today, it feels good to be tame, and besides, who else but I need know? I sleep, and by your side I dream of things I never knew I wanted, and before dawn I slip away back into my own skin, for to travel too far can be dangerous, and we may never find ourselves again if we stay away too long. I slip into my own skin, and lying on my bracken bed, I think of William, and smile, and look up at the waning moon under the tapestry of the sky.

Five

Today, I am a wild brown goat upon the craggy mountainside. Down in the village, I can see the shepherd with his flock on the hill; the farmer with his plough horse. Down by the church, there's a wedding, with bridey-cake and garlands. *Marry in May, you'll regret it for aye.* And yet the bride seems happy enough in her veil like a beekeeper's net. Both are keepers of the hive. Both shall have their honey.

Every night this week I have spent sleeping by William's bedside. Instead of hunting with the owl or running with the vixen, I have been a tabby cat, purring, playful and content, watching William as he sleeps, sitting in his lap as he reads, accepting morsels from his hand. And now I know that this feeling is not a curse, or a spell, or a dream. It is as real as the starry sky, and the hot blood of the rat I caught last night in the castle kitchens. This feeling, at once so strong and so sweet; so real, and yet insubstantial. I have been warned against it, and yet it does not seem so dangerous. And besides, my William is not at all like the other young men of the Folk. William is kind, and good, and passionate, and caring. William does not belong behind stone walls and battlements. And William is lonely, and wild, and longs for someone to care for.

As I crop the heather a kestrel calls from the open sky: *Stay away. Stay away!* She means it as a warning. The travelling folk are quick to learn of any breach of the laws of our kind. Mine is not an offence – not yet – but it is a cause for concern. *Stay away*, shrieks the kestrel. *Stay away from William MacCormac.*

I have heard this warning many times over the past days. It comes to me from the sheep on the fells; from the hare in the long grass; even from the wild bees in the forest canopy. *Bees, bees, your master is dead. Will ye work for the new one?*

I shake my horns at the kestrel. I do not need its warning. I'll go to the castle as I please, and no William shall snare me. I shall go into a cat, and sleep on his pillow all night long. Not because he is my love, but because I do as I please, and no one tells me what to do. And maybe because of that warm hearth, and the coverlet all silk and gold, and the scent of him, and his hands on my fur, and his voice like antler-velvet—

High on the rocks, a mockery of crows takes up the warning. *Beware!* But I am already on my way, travelling first into a fox, and then into a warbler, and then into the purring cat, while out in the night, the owl screams – *Fool! Love-tamed fool!* – and the mice, growing fat and bold, dance in the dying firelight.

June

The Rose Month

†

Sumer is icumen in
Lhude sing cuccu
Groweþ sed
and bloweþ med
and springþ þe wde nu
Sing cuccu –

Cuckoo song: 13th century

One

Today I am a skylark, tumbling high among the clouds, flinging my song against the peaks, dancing with the rainbows. Who could have known love would be like this? Why did no one tell me?

Last night I was a tabby cat, just like every night last week. I slept on William's pillow and purred, and watched him as he slumbered. But I was no longer content. I wanted more than this. And why not? Why should I alone be denied something that any village girl can know? Our kind have so many powers. Why should love be forbidden? And so, at last, I came to my love, not as a fox, or a nightingale, but as myself, in my own skin, warm and brown and naked. He opened his eyes and looked at me. His eyes were summer in a glass.

'How can you be here?' he said. 'Are you a fairy, or a dream?'

I shook my head.

'I have dreamed of you,' he said, 'since the day I first saw you. You stepped out of the trees like a forest doe. And then you were gone just as suddenly, and I thought I would go mad with wanting you.'

'I was never gone,' I said. 'I was here all the time.'

And then the heat was upon me, not as a doe, or a wolf, or a lynx, but – and for the first time – as a woman.

So, this is love, I told myself, as berry-brown and petal-pale we lay together flank to flank. And with his hands, and with his mouth, he made me sing like a nightingale, and soar like an eagle, and howl like a wolf, and scream and squall like a mountain cat.

'Who are you?' he said, when at last we were spent. 'Tell me your name, at least, so that I can write it on my heart.'

I smiled, and did not answer.

'But how will I find you again?' he said. 'For I must see you again, or die.'

'I'll be here,' I told him, 'for as long as there are fish in the sea, and stars in the sky, and birds in the air, and dreams in the hearts of the Folk.'

He said: 'That isn't long enough.' And then he

kissed me and I soared like a lark, and came down laughing and filled with love, and swore I would be his for ever.

Two

Today I must gather wood and supplies. For three days my hut has stood empty. For three days my firepit has been cold, and my willow traps have gone unchecked. I know all this because I travelled into a roe deer this morning, and saw the coloured things by my door shining in the sunlight, and the white-headed crow perched by the door, and heard its harsh-voiced warning. And this morning, a great black dog came to sit by my bedside, and when I looked into its eyes, it growled and said: *Come home. Come home.*

But William does not want me to leave. 'What do I care for your hut?' he says. 'What do I care for your willow traps? My home is a castle. You are its queen. You will eat roast guinea fowl, and strawberries from my hothouse. You will drink the finest wines, and taste the most delicate pastries.'

I try to explain that my people have different – wilder – ways to the Folk. We make our bed under the gorse, and travel with the seasons. We have no home, no family, not even a name to bind us.

'Then take *my* name,' says William. 'My house is proud and noble. I will share my name with you if only you will stay with me. My father is a wealthy man, gone to fight a foreign war. When he dies – which may be soon – I shall inherit his fortune. You shall have gold, and silks, and furs. You shall have horses and servants. You shall have everything you desire, if only you will stay with me.'

I have no need of silks and furs. I have no need of servants. I have the silk of the dragonfly's wing, the snowy coat of the winter hare. I have the gold of the morning sun, the colours of the Northlights. And I can go into a horse, and run across the marshlands, or travel with the wild geese as they fly towards the sun—

But I can say none of this to my love, who looks at me so tenderly. And so I promise to stay, and he laughs, and pulls me into bed once more, and draws the curtains around us like the tent of a travelling chieftain, and tells me I am his bonny brown girl, and that he would rather die than be parted from me.

Three

'You are my bonny brown girl,' he says. It is the first time that I have known anyone call me beautiful. My people are not beautiful, not as the Folk understand it. We have no love for artifice. We do not try to change ourselves into what we should not be.

Not for us the scented oils, plucked eyebrows, ironed hair. Not for us the shaven leg, the corset, comb and mirror. Not for us, the curling pins, the powder and the rouge pot. For my William, I would try. I would pretend to be tame, if it meant I could stay by his side. But my hair is a blackberry tangle impossible to comb through. My eyes are black, my brows are thick, my body strong and sturdy. And William loves the fine black silk that lines my legs and armpits, and the roundness of my breasts, and the soft broad curve of my hip, and would not see me change a thing.

Except that here, in his castle, if I am to be seen by his folk without causing a scandal, I need to wear suitable clothing, and bathe, and learn to read my letters, and dress my hair in the manner of those village girls I so despise.

'When my father returns from the wars,' he says, 'I want him to cherish you as I do.'

'And would you cherish me more,' I ask, 'in velvet than in wolfskin?'

'Velvet or wolfskin, homespun or silk, you will always be my love. But my people must respect you. I want them to call you My Lady. I want them to serve you as they serve me. And besides,' he says, taking me in his arms, 'just imagine how much more beautiful you will be in a gown of silk, with pearls at your throat, and satin slippers on your feet?'

And so I accepted, to please him. What harm can it do, after all, to pretend? When I travel as a hawk, I do so in borrowed plumage. How is this any different? And when I take off my borrowed clothes, and lie with him, I will always be his wild brown girl from the forest.

He found me a maid from the village. The maid is called Fiona. A rose-pink, cowslip, buttercup girl, without a hint of wildness. He brought her here to wait on me, to lay out my clothes and brush my hair, but I can see the look in her eyes, and I know that she despises me. And sometimes I catch her looking at him, and I know that she is thinking: *What does he see in a nameless brown girl? How has she bewitched him?*

But William does not see it. He says: 'Fiona is a good girl. She will teach you all you need.'

This makes me angry. How can he believe that girl could possibly teach me anything? Does Fiona know how to catch a salmon with her bare hands? Does she know how to soar with the lark, or climb to the eagle's eyrie? Does she know how to make a charm blacker than the darkest night, to steal the soul of her enemy?

He sees the look in my eyes and says: 'Poor Fiona. Surely you are not jealous of her?'

I turn away and will not speak.

'That mooncalf? That dough-faced ninny?' he says. 'That sighing, simpering little miss, not fit to kiss my lady's feet?'

I laugh at the absurdity. The wild folk do not envy the tame. I feel ashamed that William thinks me capable of such thoughts, and I take him in my arms, and laugh, and tell him how much I love him. And so, Fiona is with me now every hour of every day. She wakes me in the morning with a cup of chocolate. She fetches water for my bath, and scents it with rose oil and lavender. She brings me books from the castle library, and helps me to make out the words. She brings me clothes and jewellery belonging to William's dead mother. I wear a dress of crimson velvet, with petticoats of scarlet silk, and my hair is caught in a jewelled net, and my feet crammed into high-heeled shoes. There are rings on my fingers, and bracelets all along my arms. This way, William tells me, I can live in the castle without alerting suspicion. This way, I look like a lady, he says, and not a brown girl from the woods.

'But I *am* a brown girl from the woods,' I say, laughing, in spite of my unease.

But my William does not laugh. Instead he looks very serious. I must make an effort, he says. The servants are bound to his father. *He* is the laird of the castle, and they will relay any news to him. This is why I must dress like a lady, and have a maidservant with me, and learn to read, and to use a fork, and not to run, or shout, or laugh.

'If you really loved me,' he says, 'you would do this for my sake. Instead, you treat it like a game. Understand that if my father does not approve of my lady-love, he will cut me off without a penny. Is that what you want?'

'Of course not,' I say. And yet my heart aches. Why

does he care so much for these things? Castle walls, and servants, and gold are nothing compared to our freedom. We could have the moors, and the lakes, and the open skies, and the mountains. We could live in the forest, alone, and be everything to each other. But William, I know, would miss the comfort of his home, and hearth, and his bed with the silken coverlet. And it makes him so happy to have me here. I must not be ungrateful.

But, for all their obedience and calling me *My Lady*, I know that the servants despise me. I have seen them watching me, and once I went into a rat that lives in a hole by the pantry door, and heard one of the chefs discussing me with the Master of the Wines.

'She's no more than a hoor,' said the chef, 'for all her fine clothes and trinkets.'

'I heard she was a witch,' replied the Master of Wines with a leer. 'How else could such as she get her claws into young Master William?'

'Young Master William,' said the chef, 'is barely nineteen summers old. A boy should sow his wild oats, but not in his father's castle.'

'I've heard he means to make her his bride,' said the Master of Wines.

The chef shook his head. 'A boy's fancy. The moment

the master comes home, mark my words, the baggage will be on her way.'

That made me angry, and I fled from the rat into a wolf, and found a herd of penned sheep in the glen, and tore out their white throats one by one, but got no relief from it, even though my coat was drenched and crimson with their innocent blood, and when I returned to myself, I found the maid Fiona watching me with a curious look on her face, as if she knew more than she meant to tell.

And so after that I was careful not to travel, except at night. It was hard. I miss being free. But I can bear it, for William. I would give up everything for him, as I know he would for me, if I were to ask him. And as the rose month reaches its peak, and midsummer is upon us, I know that our joy will grow and grow, and fill the earth with roses.

Four

Today is Midsummer's Day, the day when travelling folk come together to celebrate the green month: not as winged and dappled things, but as ourselves, all brown and wild, selling our goods at the Midsummer Fair.

On Midsummer's Fair Day in the town square, there will be honey, and ribbons, and fruit. There will be baskets, and cages of birds. There will be potions, and magic spells, and charms to summon your true love. There will be dancing on the green, and even the Folk of the village will come, half-afraid, half-longing – to buy, to gaze, to envy, to scorn – to the gathering of the travelling folk.

I have never yet missed a fair. But this time, I am afraid to go. The messages from the owl, the crow, the kestrel and the black dog have given way to a silence more ominous than their warnings. I cannot make them understand how much my William means to me. But William wants to go to the Fair. He wants to show his brown girl the town, with its fine buildings and towers of stone. And the maid Fiona has told him of all the many things to be bought, and he has promised me a gift, a special gift from the market.

'But I already have jewels and gowns, and shoes, and combs, and picture-books. What more do I need?'

He smiles at me. Those things belonged to his mother, he says. He has so little of his own. Until he comes of age, he has only a small allowance. And yet he wants to buy me a gift, a gift to show his love for me.

'When I come of age,' he says, 'I shall be a wealthy man. I shall buy you a singing bird in a cage of ivory. I shall buy you a swarm of bees in a fortress of honey-comb. I shall buy you a golden ring to wear upon your finger.'

A golden ring, to show the world that he is mine and I am his. So much for the castle chef and the Master of Wines. *A June bride is impetuous and open-handed*, say the Folk. I shall be a June bride, and dance on the green in my wedding veil, and throw rose petals and bridey-cakes to the children in the crowd. And all the village girls will wonder why, of all the girls he might have picked, the wild girl was the one he chose.

And so I take my William's hand, and smile, and say, 'Of course, my love,' because I want to please him, but also because I want *them* to see how happy we are together, I in my dress of red velvet, he in his coat of summer-sky blue, walking, gracious, hand in hand, like the King and Queen of Fiddler's Green.

The black dog watches in silence. The kestrel soars without a word. And William calls for his coach and four, and his man (and the maid Fiona, of course), and together we ride to the market. And as we go, I sing to myself, a little song of the travelling folk:

Sing a song of starlight,
A pocketful of crows.
See the bonny brown girl
In her borrowed clothes.
See her in a vixen,
See her in a hare,
See her in her true love's arms, at sweet Midsummer's
fair.

Five

The town is sixteen miles away: two hours at a fast trot. The day is warm, and I find myself sweating in my velvet. Oh, to be a doe today, in the cool glades of the forest. Or an otter by the lake, or a salmon in the stream. But I dare not travel here, not with William by my side, and the maid Fiona watching every move I make.

And so I watch the countryside, and pretend to listen as William tells me all about the town – a town I know as well as he does, for I have seen it many times as a bird, or a dog, or a horse, although I cannot tell him that, for fear of betraying my people. Maybe when we are married, I will. Married folk share everything.

At last, we reach the marketplace. A cobbled square, with a fountain, around which hundreds of stallholders compete with each other for custom. I know my people by sight, of course. There's one selling crows: she lives most of her life among the birds, and even now she looks more like a black bird than a woman, except for the white blaze in her hair. There's one selling tokens and charms – a cluster of bells to keep the fairies at bay; a bird's head on a willow twig to cure a bishop of the pox; a vial of rainbow water to cure a miser of his misery. And there's another – old as Old Age, with skin as hard and brown and cracked as an ancient hawthorn tree – selling strings of coloured beads: turquoise, beryl, amethyst; quartz and pearl and ruby.

William stops by the old woman's stall. 'How much for these?'

Her eyes are as bright as the lake, and as cold. 'For this young lady, no charge,' she says. 'For what we give freely on Midsummer's Day will return to us a hundredfold.' And she reaches out her misshapen hand and brings back a necklace of tiger's-eye beads, brown and gold in the sunlight.

'Wear this, my beauty,' she whispers, as she fastens the clasp around my neck. 'The gold in your eyes is truer by far than the gold he promised you.'

I thank her, though she has troubled me. Is she suggesting he could be false? I know him better. My love is true. The old woman means to frighten me, but I shall not heed her. Instead, I laugh a little too loudly, pretend to look at some rolls of silk, and tug at the tiger's-eye necklace, which feels as if it is choking me, then laugh again, take William's hand, and try not to see the wild dark faces watching me from every stall, the wild dark eyes alight with scorn—

We drive back in silence. William rides. Fiona, too, has a necklace. Hers is made of crystal quartz, as white as a string of snowdrops. William bought it as a gift, he says, to thank her for coming so far with us. This does not disturb me. The necklace is a cheap thing, as colourless as Fiona herself. And yet I do not like the way she smiles to herself as she handles the beads, pressing her fingers against her breast as if at some re-membered touch. I do not like the way she looks with downcast eyes at William. I do not like her primrose hair, which makes me remember the village girl who hung the charm on the fairy tree—

Could that have been Fiona? I never saw the other girl's face. *She* could have stitched the silken charm, and passed it through the adder-stone, and hung it onto the fairy tree. Does she suspect that I stole the charm? Could that be why she hates me?

Well, if she does, what of it? My love has pledged himself to me. I know his heart, as he knows mine.

I need no charm to capture him; no adder-stone to watch him by. William will be true to me. Whatever else happens – he will be true.

July

The Hay Month

✝

A swarm of bees in May
Is worth a load of hay,
A swarm of bees in June
Is worth a silver spoon,
A swarm of bees in July
Is not worth a fly.

17th-century proverb

One

I shall bind my love with silk, as red as summer roses.
I shall bind my love with runes as secret as the dreams
of the Folk. I shall bind my love with whitethorn, and
rue, and rosemary, and ivy leaf, and honeysuckle, and
tie it up into a charm to keep my lover faithful.

Not that I doubt my William. Our love is like the
mountains. Our love is like the stormy sea. Our love
is like the midnight sky. But the old woman's words
still trouble me, and I miss my freedom. Last night I
went into an owl, and hunted mice in the castle's dry
moat. I dare not travel too far from here, in case I am
discovered. But I miss the peaks and the cold black
lake, and the forest, and the islands. I miss the open
sky, and the sun, and the song of the morning in my
throat.

And William still does not understand why I cannot give him my name. 'You must have a name,' he says one day. 'All God's creatures have a name.'

But I am *not* one of his creatures. My people are older than your God. My people were here when these mountains were ice, and these valleys were nothing but streamlets running down from the glacier. I have been every bird, every beast, every insect you can name. And so I have no name of my own, and cannot be tamed or commanded. But I can say none of this to William, who looks at me so earnestly.

'You call me your bonny brown girl. I need no other name,' I say.

'And will my father name you thus, when he comes home from the wars? And at our wedding, must the parson say: *I join thee together in matrimony, William John Makepeace MacCormac and . . . a bonny brown girl?*

The bride of July is handsome, but quick and sharp of temper. I do not want to be sharp of temper, and yet what can I say to him, when he teases and presses me so?

'I do not have a name,' I say. 'My people have no need of them.'

But this time William will not stop. 'Is your name Amanda?' he says. 'Amanda is *Beloved*. Or Ailsa, *Noble Maiden*? Or Morag, which means *Princess*?'

'And Fiona?' Slyly: 'What does that mean?'

'It means *White Lady*.'

I should have known. *The bride of July is handsome, but quick and sharp of temper*. I turn away so that he cannot see the glowering of my black brows.

He laughs and takes me in his arms. 'Surely, you are not jealous of poor Fiona?' he tells me. 'Does the sun envy the dandelion? Does the star envy the firefly?'

I shake my head.

He laughs again. 'But I cannot wed a nameless girl. I shall name you Malmuira – *Dark Lady of the Mountains*. Thus are you named, my brown girl. Thus do you belong to me.' And with that, he kisses me, and laughs, little knowing that with one word he has bound me faster than any charm of the Faërie.

Two

I shall bind my love with salt, and lead, and penny-royal. I shall bind him with spider silk, and pudding grass, and larkspur, and with the sound of a moon moth against a windowpane at night, and with the taste of a memory that has soured into smoke.

A named thing is a tamed thing. So says the lore of my people. A named thing keeps the hearth, the home. A named thing has a master. And now, for the first time, *I* have a name. Malmuira. *Dark Lady.* I wear it like a golden crown. I wear it like a collar.

Tonight I feel restless. I want to run. I want to fly, and hunt, and swim. I will go into a crane, and fly over the marshlands. I will go into a bear, and fish for salmon in the lake. I will go into a vixen—

But I cannot free my mind. The crane flies on without

me. The bear hunts upriver, shaking his head. The vixen raids the chicken coop and crosses the meadows without me. My head is on fire. What sickness is this? The maid Fiona brings me a draught. But I want to be alone to shed this skin and be free of myself. Perhaps I am overreaching my skills. A housecat, then, or a mouse, or a bat. I shall nest under the eaves. I shall run through the stone halls. I shall feel the clean night air and look up at the naked stars—

Still, I cannot free myself. My dress, with its bodice, feels like a cage. The silver mesh around my hair feels like a fishing net lined with lead. The tiger's-eye necklace around my throat has become a bridle of hot stones. I want to tear myself free of it all, but I cannot. I have a name. It binds me. I am no longer a child of the world, no longer one of the travelling folk, but a named thing. A girl called Malmuira.

For a time, I cannot think. I am a wild bird in a snare. I am a fox in a steel trap. I want to scream, to bite, to run. But all I can do is sit quietly, by the window, and stare at the sky. My William calls me for dinner. There will be a roasted fowl, and artichokes, and many wines. There will be a raised apple pie, and comfits, and cherries and peaches. I shall wear a yellow silk gown, with rings of gold on my fingers, and the servants will bow very low, and call me *My Lady*, with that sneer that they hide behind their hands, and think: *Is that your name, My Lady? Can that really be your name?*

I tell him I am not hungry. I will not go to dinner. He looks displeased but says nothing, and goes to dine without me. I wish I could tell him how I feel. But that would mean giving away secrets that are not mine to give. I cannot betray my heart, my blood. The travelling folk may have disowned me, but they are still my people.

Three

Last night it rained, and the sound of it was like a stream with a throatful of stones. And in my dream I remembered the adder-stone I had thrown away, and tried to find it in the stream, so I could see William. But the stream was filled with pieces of glass, which cut my hands and made them bleed, and soon the water was nothing but blood, dark and hot and crimson—

I awoke from my troubled sleep to the sound of voices. William was not at my side. I rose, and went to open the door. There was a light in the passageway. I saw a man in outdoor clothes carrying a lantern, and William with his back to me. The maid Fiona was at his side, wearing a dress of grey cambric, her unbound hair falling down her back, and I felt a small, sharp stab at the way she looked at him through her lashes.

'What's happening?' I said.

William glanced back at me. It may have been the light, but for a moment I thought he looked annoyed. Not at me. Never at me. But something must have happened.

William did not speak to me, but gestured for me to go back inside. I was barefoot, in my nightgown. My hair was wild. I understood. I went back into our bedroom and I waited for William to come. But hours passed, and he did not, although I heard his voice from outside, and the sound of horses in the court-yard. Someone had arrived. I heard at least a dozen horses.

I would have gone into a bird, to see what the commotion was. But I could not. Nor could I travel into a rat, and listen from inside the walls. And so I waited until dawn, when Fiona came to dress me and to bring me my chocolate and the hot water for my toilette.

But this morning there was no hot water. Nor was there any chocolate, in its little bone-china cup with a honey-cake on the side, or a piece of shortbread. Instead the maid Fiona brought me a plain green cambric dress and a dish of porridge, and brushed my hair only long enough to secure it under a plain white cap, and all the time she was looking at me from under those long eyelashes, as if to say: *I know your kind. You are not of our kind. The Master may not know it, but I do.*

I did not ask about the dress, or the missing choco-late. I said nothing as I washed my face and hands in cold water. The maid Fiona sat and watched, and did not offer to help me. Then, as I reached for the bracelets and rings that I had taken off for the night, she said to me in her milkwater voice:

'The Master desires me to take those back. They were My Lady's, and should not have left her chambers.'

I was surprised, but said nothing. Instead I put on my tiger's-eye beads, and wished I could be a tiger. If I were a tiger, I would tear out the throats of village girls; of cornsilk, buttermilk, cottontail girls. I would tear out their white throats, and dance in the rain all cloaked in their blood. Of course I cannot do those things. But I can still wear my tiger's-eye beads, which my William gave to me, and smile although my heart is lead, and I do not feel like smiling. My William will come to me soon. My William will explain all this.

Fiona went out, with that look of hers, like a cat with its face in the cream-pot. I threw the cold por-ridge onto the floor, and tried to read the storybook that was lying on the table. It was about a handsome P-R-I-N-C-E, who falls in love with a P-R-I-N-C-E-S-S. But she has been cursed by a W-I-C-K-E-D W-I-T-C-H, and made to scrub floors in his father's kitchens. The stupid prince does not recognise her when he goes in search of her. But a G-O-O-D F-A-I-R-Y, moved by her plight, gives the girl three wishes. The princess asks for a fine silk gown, and some dancing shoes, and a coach with four white horses, all so that the prince will notice her. And sure enough, now that she is beautiful, he marries her, and gives her a veil, and a gold ring to put on her finger to show that she belongs to him, and, with his father's blessing, they live H-A-P-P-I-L-Y E-V-E-R A-F-T-E-R.

It is a ridiculous story. The prince should have recognised his love whatever she was wearing. Even dressed as a bird, or a rat, or snake, or a fox, or a weasel, his heart should have told him she was there. And why did the princess not speak out when the prince went looking for her? Why did she lurk in the kitchens, waiting to be saved? Why could she not save herself? And what does the prince's father have to do with anything? And why would one of the Faërie have given her three wishes? And why would she waste them on a dress, some dancing shoes and a coach and four?

Perhaps the pictures in the book will shed some light on the story. But the princess in the pictures looks just like Fiona: a village girl with primrose hair and a pale, round, milkweed face. The prince is not much better.

But the wicked witch is brown, all dressed in rags and feathers. The wicked witch has wild black hair, and eyes as black as cauldrons.

I wonder what the village girl did to offend the wicked witch. Did she simply look at her in that sly, contemptuous way, as if to say: *I know your kind*? Or was it something even worse?

I look at myself in the mirror. Even with my wild hair caught beneath the little cap, I still look like the wicked witch. I take off the cap and shake my hair free. The tiger's-eye necklace is choking me, and I would like to take off, but it was William's gift to me, and so I endure the discomfort.

But was it *really* William's gift? *What we give freely on Midsummer's Day will return to us a hundredfold.* And now I remember the old woman's words as she clasped it around my neck: *The gold in your eyes is truer by far than the gold he promised you—*

It was noon before Fiona came back. She saw the broken dish on the floor and the picture-book beside it. She gave me a look – for the first time, eye to eye, like an equal. Her eyes are blue, like forget-me-nots, and bolder than I expected. I noticed that she was wearing the necklace William bought for her, and I wanted to tear it from her neck, scatter the beads across the floor, mark her face with my fingernails. Fiona saw the look in my eyes and gave a smile, as if to say: *I know what you want to do. But you will not, because you are tamed.*

And then she said in her milksop voice: 'The Master sends his compliments, and bids me tell you he has important family business to attend to. Regrettably, this means that he can no longer extend his hospitality to guests. He hopes that you will understand, and wishes you a pleasant homeward journey.'

I stared at her for a moment. 'William said this?' I said, forgetting in my rage and astonishment to say *Master William*.

'Not the *young* Master,' she said. ''Twas the *Master* bade me tell you.'

'The Master?' I said, feeling foolish.

'Yes,' she said with a little smile. 'John MacCormac has come home.'

Four

I walked home by the high road, avoiding the track to the village. At another time, I would have travelled as a magpie, or maybe as a mountain goat, or crossed the lake as a wild duck, before joining the deer in the forest. But this time I had to walk, and although I carried my high-heeled shoes, it took me most of the rest of the day to return to my hut in the forest.

It has been too long since I slept on my bed of bracken and wool. Too long since I used my cooking pot, or dried my meat in the campfire smoke. The roof of my hut has partly collapsed under the weight of a fallen branch. Some animal has been inside. My blanket is wet and spotted with mould. And my coloured things – my ribbons and beads – have been plundered from my door. Maybe a magpie, I tell myself. Or maybe just a white-headed crow.

As I work to make the hut habitable again, I tell myself that William will come. As soon as he can, he will come to me, and we will be together again. And is this not what I wanted? To be with my love in the forest, with the trees as our castle walls and the stars for our ceiling?

I try to keep merry. I sing to myself, but somehow the words sound hollow.

Sing a song of starlight,
A pocket full of crows.
See the bonny brown girl
In her borrowed clothes—

What am I doing here, William? Night is falling. Too late to hunt. Too late to gather fiddleheads. Besides, the season is over now: the ferns have grown tall in my absence. How long has it been? The bluebells are dry; the May buds have gone. Above the lake, the July sky is all aflame in pink and gold. I wonder if William sees the same sky from his rooms in the castle. How worried he must be, I think. How he must long to be with me. But his father is home now, and William is bound to obey. I must be patient. I must not let my anger run free. When his business is done, then perhaps John MacCormac will see me. He will see me, and understand how much my William means to me. Why else would I have stayed by his side, and worn fine gowns to please him? Why else would I have taken a name, and abandoned the ways of the travelling folk?

And if he does *not* understand—

If he does not, my love will come and live with me in the forest. It will be hard for him at first, but has he not told me a hundred times? *I would rather live in a hut with you, than in a palace without you. I would rather die than be a single night away from you.*

Well, we may be a night apart. But no one can part us for ever. Tomorrow, I shall rebuild my hut, to prepare for your arrival. I shall build it from green oak, and thatch it with reeds from the lakeside. I shall line it with rabbit skins, and moss, and fern, and heather. I shall catch salmon, and smoke them, and pick green plums from the orchards, and apples from the churchyard, and wild oats from the edge-lands. I shall make you a blanket from the very softest lambswool, and dye it in the colours of love: crimson, blue and purple. And if your father will not relent, then we will live in the forest alone, and gather berries, and hunt the deer, and sleep throughout the winter snow in each other's arms. And if I never have a veil, or a golden ring on my hand, I will still have you, my love, and that will be enough for me. Sleep well, love, and dream of me. And know that, if I were to live for a thousand years, there would still not be enough nights in which to dream of you.

August

The Harvest Month

✝

My love he was so high and proud,
His fortune too so high,
He for another fair pretty maid
Me left and passed me by.

The Child Ballads, 295

One

It has been a week since I left, without a word from William. Of course, he does not know where I am, or how to find me in the woods. But I know he will, soon. How I wish I could see him. How I wish I could go to him, even as a housecat. But I cannot go into even the humblest creature. Not an ant, not a frog, not a beetle will grant me passage into their skin.

An August bride is sweet-tempered and active. I have tried my best to be so. My hut is all lined with fresh new moss, and strewn with summer roses. I lay down clean rushes every day. I hunt for thrush, and trout in the stream, and pick blackberries and wild strawberries, to prepare for the coming of my love.

But he does not come. Where can he be? No one passes through the glen. There comes no sound of horses' hooves on the road from the castle. Why has he left me waiting so long? Surely he must know where I am! Is he ill? Is he bewitched? Or could he have forgotten me?

No. That would be impossible. Our love is as strong as the mountains, as endless as the oceans. Maybe he is testing me. Maybe this is a test to see how much more I will endure for him.

I have never needed my gift as badly as I need it now. To go into a bird, a hare – even for an hour – would tell me all I need to know. And yet I cannot. How can that be? And how can I make things right again?

Last night, I went to the fairy tree, the oldest of our people. She rarely leaves her hawthorn skin, except once a year, for the market. But I know she watches, and I hoped she could help me.

I found her in the meadow mist, her feet already drenched with dew. Around her, the stones looked like islands rising out of the pale mist. Only one of her branches still lives, and the fruit that grows there is sparse and green. I wondered how old she really is: some of the travelling folk believe that she is more than nine hundred years old, and was born at a time when travelling folk covered all of the Nine Worlds. Now we are few, growing fewer, as the tame folk multiply.

The branches of the fairy tree were covered in rags and ribbons. The hawthorn loves her trinkets, and must always be paid for her charms. Love charms, mostly, of course, with a bird's skull to ward off the plague, a silver spoon for childbirth. They clicked together as the wind took hold of them, as if the tree were a toothless old crone smacking her gums in the moonlight.

I whispered: 'Can you hear me?'

The hawthorn ticked and fluttered. Over her head, the Barley Moon sharpened her silver sickle.

'I need your help,' I told her. 'My power to travel has left me.'

There came a snickering, whispering sound, almost like distant laughter.

Left you? said the hawthorn tree in a sighing, creaking voice. *You were the one who stopped listening. You gave us up, for a boy of the Folk. For a handful of pretty pebbles. For the promise of a ring.*

'That isn't true,' I protested.

A named thing is a tamed thing, said the voice from the hawthorn tree. *You let the boy give you a name. How can you live among wild things again?*

'There must be a way,' I told her.

Oh, there's a way, said the hawthorn tree. *But it won't be easy.*

'Tell me,' I said.

One thing at a time. Wisdom must always be paid for. Give me those fine shoes you wear, and I will give you my advice.

I kicked off my shoes and hung them on the hawthorn's living branch. They were leather, and finely made, with silver buckles and scarlet heels, but I only wore them for William's sake, and my feet felt better without them.

'Take them with my blessing,' I said. 'Now tell me what I must do.'

The hawthorn made a contented sound. *First give away all he has given you*, she said. *Give away every stitch, every word, every bead, every sigh, every promise. And when you are free of it all, then your name will melt away like the spring snow, and you will be free of him again, and able to travel as you please.*

'But I don't want to be free of him,' I said. 'Is there no other way?'

She sighed. *How can you fly with a stone around your neck? How can you run with a chain on your feet?*

'But I love him,' I said.

That's the stone. That's the chain, said the hawthorn. *And until you can give them back, you will never be free again.*

I sighed. 'So be it, Old Mother. Better to live in

chains with my love than to travel freely without him.'

She laughed. *We'll see about that*, she said. *Go back to your cold bed. Think about what I told you. You may change your mind before too long. And thank you for the pretty shoes. Even an old woman like me likes her tricks and trinkets.* The ribbons and charms on her branches clinked and fluttered coquettishly. Not for the first time, I wondered if she remembered the adder-stone charm; if this was her way of punishing me for taking what belonged to her. But I could not return it now, or even beg her pardon. The charm was burnt, and the adder-stone given back to the water.

And so I went back home barefoot through the woods, to my empty hut, and my aching heart, and the bitter smoke from my campfire.

Two

At last, a letter from William. I found it this morning by my hut, underneath a hazel tree. There was a white-headed crow by the tree, pecking at the envelope. I tried to talk to the white-headed crow, but all she said was: *Letter*. And such was my joy at receiving it that I opened it straight away, and when I had read it, the crow was gone.

I read:

> *My dear M-A-L-M-U-I-R-A,*
> *Forgive me for not having come to see you. My father is recently back from the wars, and there is much B-U-S-I-N-E-S-S to conduct.*

His writing was difficult to make out. There were

many flourishes and curlicues in the letters. But I could read it, given time, and besides, it was in his own dear hand, with words that he had chosen for me.

Do not think I have F-O-R-G-O-T-T –

Of course. I could never think that.

It is simply that we may have to be more P-A-T-I-E-N-T than I first hoped. My father is a difficult man. I must try to A-P-P-E-A-S-E him before you meet him in person. I am not yet come of age, or into my I-N-H-E-R-I-T-A-N-C-E. I must gain his A-P-P-R-O-V-A-L before I think of M-A-R-R-I-A-G-E.

I feel certain that, given time, I can make him U-N-D-E-R-S-T-A-N-D. You are my only love, and I cannot live without you.

But until then, I shall send F-I-O-N-A to carry my messages, and to bring you whatever you may need. She is a good girl, D-E-V-O-T-E-D to me, and you may trust her to be D-I-S-C-R-E-E-T.

Your ever-faithful,
W-I-L-L-I-A-M.

I supposed Fiona had left the note by the hut in my absence. When I returned, I also found a neatly wrapped parcel of bread and cheese, some honey and a basket of fruit, standing by the firepit. She must have left them here for me, while the white-headed crow watched from the trees.

Fiona. That pat-a-cake village girl. I hate the thought of her coming here, nosing about outside my door. How did she know where to find me? Do the villagers know where I am? And why did William send her, instead of coming here himself?

Of course, I know why. These things take time. He said we must be patient. And he thinks of me. That's good.

And yet I still wish he had come here himself, with or without his father's approval. It reminds me somehow of that storybook, and the prince who did not recognise his love when she worked in the kitchens.

Well, I am not a kitchen princess, to hide away and pine for love. If my William does not come, then I will go to him myself. And if anyone tries to keep us apart—

Beware the wrath of a brown girl.

Three

I shall bind my love with smoke, and moss, and eagle feathers. I shall bind him with runes so strong that even Death will shun him. I shall bind him by his name and mine – the name that has already cost me so much – both stitched into a piece of cloth and carried next to my heart, so that however many miles lie between us, we shall never be apart.

Fiona came again today, but this time I was waiting. She brought some bread, some honey-cakes, and some milk, some cheese, and a pitcher of wine. There was no note from William. But her cat-in-the-cream look was enough to make me suspicious. Could she have stolen his letter? Could she be trying to steal something more?

I have written a note of my own. It took me four

days, using an eagle-feather quill and on paper made from dried flowers. I kept it to a single page, and sealed it with a candle-stub. It read:

Dear WILLIAM,
Thank You for your Note, and the Parcel, although it is Your own Self, and not Provisions, that I need. I miss You so much that my Heart Aches, and wish I could be with You. Do not send FIONA. I have never trusted her. Instead, I shall come to You tomorrow at Noon, and meet You in the Kitchens, where No One will Trouble our Meeting. Till then,
Your Love,
Malmuira.

Malmuira. How strange to write that name. It does not feel like a part of me. And yet it was a gift from him, a gift that I could not refuse. Now I have made him a gift in return: a sachet, stitched with both our names and filled with purple lavender, a token of love for William when I see him tomorrow.

Fiona took the note with a smirk. But I know she cannot open it without breaking the waxen seal. If she does, my William will know. If she does not, no matter.

And now, all I must do is wait until tomorrow. Tomorrow I will see him again. Tomorrow, in the kitchens.

Four

I shall bind my love with the cry of a snowy owl in the darkness. I shall bind him with nightshade, and the collarbone of a moon hare. I shall bind him in a sheet made from stars and thistledown, and sleep with him for a thousand years, until the seas are nothing but sand, and the mountains are nothing but ocean.

I took the high road through the hills towards my William's castle. I wore the dress he gave me, with my tiger's-eye necklace around my neck, and my hair fastened back with a strand of silk, all tied with purple clover. The sun was already high in the sky, and the hills were garlanded with rainbows. I took it as a good sign:

Rainbow at morn,
Put your hook in the corn.

Rainbow at eve,
Put your head in the sheave.

I even sang to myself as I walked along the heathery path through the hills; not as a lark, but as myself, and my voice startled the grouse on the moor, so that they flew out a-clattering.

At noon I went to the kitchen door, and waited for William to come. But no one came, and finally I had to ring the bell.

One of the potboys answered. His eyes went wide as he saw me. Then he ran to fetch the chef – the same one who had called me a hoor – who looked at me from a height and said: 'There's nothing here for you, miss.'

'Master William knows I am here,' I said. 'I wrote to him only yesterday.'

The chef gave a shrug. 'If he knows you're here, then why is he not here to greet you? And why come here, to the kitchen door, like a servant or a thief?'

I shook my head. I was angry. Not with William – not yet – but with the situation. Had Fiona delivered my note? Did William even know I was here? Had he not seen me coming? Would he not have known me as I came across the moors?

'Listen, miss.' Now the look of contempt had

changed to something like pity. 'You should go home, where you belong. There's no one here.'

'That isn't true.' My voice was small, and I hated myself for not being able to go into a bear, or a wolf, or a tiger, and roar—

'There's no one here, miss. The young Master's driven off into town.'

I felt myself starting to tremble. 'Alone?'

'No, miss.' That look again: like pity mixed with sour milk.

'Who?' I said.

'His manservant, miss. And, of course, Miss Fiona.'

'I don't believe you,' I said, and now I could feel my eyes burning. I would not cry. I never cry. But the smoke from the kitchens was unbearable, and the heat from the fires was scorching, and the tears came tumbling down my cheeks before I could prevent them.

The chef said: 'I'll get you some water. And there's bread, if you're hungry.'

For a moment I was surprised at the kindness in his voice. But this was the man who had called me a hoor. I would not bear his pity. So I held my head high and walked away, my green dress trailing in the dust. Something purple fell to the ground. It was a piece of clover. Faded, it fell from the strand of silk that bound my wild hair to obedience.

And now came the anger – at him, at her, but most of all anger at myself. What a fool I have been! I thought. The hawthorn was right. He is faithless: treacherous like all of his kind, cowardly and wanton. I snatched away the piece of silk. I will have no need for it now. I am not one of your village girls, to be tamed and put aside. My power may be gone, but my rage is more than enough to sustain me. Hide behind your castle walls. Hide behind your servants. But the next time you see me, William, I shall be a tiger.

Five

Even for such as I, there are ways of finding out what needs to be known. I cannot travel, but maybe my folk can be persuaded to travel for me. The white-headed crow can be bribed with cakes: the magpie with pieces of coloured glass. And in exchange they bring me news, a whisper and a word at a time.

Fool! crows the magpie. *Faithless!* the crow. *Fiona*, whisper the reeds by the lake, and the sound is like fingernails on glass, like voices from an open grave. And today, as I sit by the firepit, I see them together, enlaced in the smoke, lily-white on petal-pale, and I know that what I see is true. My love loves another.

It rained last night, and the night before that. Wild, intemperate rain that crashes down the mountains. Oh, to go into the rain, and be lost: to go into the lightning, and strike. But I must stay in my hut alone, and watch the rain drip from the trees, and listen to the sound of the stream, and try not to dream of William.

What does he see in that cornsilk girl, that apple-blossom, goat's-milk girl? How could he have forgotten me, after all his promises? She must have used some kind of witchcraft. Lavender, for forgetfulness, a poppet made from my petticoat, and hair gathered from my brush. She knew how to make the adder-stone charm; maybe she has other skills. Perhaps I was wrong to dismiss her as just another girl of the Folk. She must be a witch, to have thwarted me. She must be a witch, to have snared him. I did not hear the knock at my door: the sound of footsteps on the path. But when I looked up, I saw a face, peering in at my window.

The travelling folk rarely show themselves, even to their own kind. There is no safety in numbers. Instead, we hunt with borrowed skin, with tooth, and horn, and antler. But this time, she had chosen to make the journey as herself, clothed in nothing but ribbons and rags, and with the fine shoes I gave her looking very out of place on her brown and knotted feet; and slowly, very slowly: for she is old as Old Age, her bones as light as driftwood, her hair a silver-moss peach-fuzz against the tender curve of her skull.

'I said you might change your mind,' she said, with a sharp-eyed glance at my face. 'I hear on the wind that your young man has found himself a fairer maid.'

I said nothing, but glared at her.

'I know a charm,' she told me, 'to help you free yourself of him.'

'I don't want to be free of *him*,' I said. 'I want him to be free of *her*.'

The hawthorn shrugged. 'That's easy. But it won't buy back *your* freedom, nor make him any less faithless.'

I shook my head. 'I don't care.'

'Very well,' said the hawthorn. 'I'll sell you a charm. But when you change your mind, come back and find me. I can help you.'

'I will not change my mind,' I said. 'Give me the charm. What's your price?'

The hawthorn smiled, her brown face all spidery with wrinkles. 'First, give me that pretty green dress you wear, to keep me warm through the winter.'

I took off the dress. It was in no way as fine as the gowns I had worn at the castle. But it was warm, and well made, and without it, I felt suddenly cold. I stood in my petticoats, shivering. The old woman put on the dress, and seemed content with the result.

'For the charm,' she said, 'you will need three

things. The first is the heartswood of an ash, drenched with nine drops of your own blood, and bound with a skein of lightning. Stitch them with the runes *Naudr* and *Thuris*, and sew them into a purse made from the shroud of an unshriven man. Leave it under her pillow, and she will have no more power over him.'

I shall bind my love with a charm made from the heartswood of an ash. I shall bind him with my blood, shed for him by moonlight. I shall bind him with the threads of lightning from the summer storms, and never let go, not for anything, not if Death himself commands it—

The hawthorn nodded and smiled. In my dress and high-heeled shoes she looked even less like one of the Folk than she had dressed in rags and feathers. Then she went on her way through the woods – slowly, very slowly – and all the forest creatures stood aside to let her pass, for the hawthorn is a cunning one, old as Old Age, and as merciless.

September

Month of White Straw

†

Me did he send a love-letter,
He sent it from the town,
Saying no more he loved me,
For that I was so brown.

The Child Ballads, 295

One

The most difficult part was finding a way to slip the charm under her pillow. She sleeps in my bedchamber now, in the bed with the silken coverlet. My messengers tell me she goes there at night, under cover of darkness, for Fiona is a virtuous maid with a good reputation.

But go there I must, I told myself, for the hawthorn's charm required it. And so I set about planning a way to gain entry into the castle. First, I needed a disguise. Clothes, stolen from a washing line. An apron, and a clean white cap, to make me look like a laundry maid. I went inside with the rest of the girls, hiding my face beneath the cap, and hid until they had all gone by, before taking a pile of clean sheets into William's chamber. It would have been easy to slip the charm into a fresh pillowcase. But I had not expected to see William there in the bedroom – William, my one true love, who had promised to love me for ever – and Fiona, in her dove-grey silk, sitting by the window.

His hair has grown since I saw him last. But he is as handsome as always. Handsome in the May Day coat he had on when first I saw him, his blue eyes filled with points of gold as he turned and looked right through me.

I felt a surge of dizziness so strong that I almost fell, but William did not notice. He looked at me, and saw me not, in spite of all I had meant to him. For what's another laundry girl, her hair bound up in a starched white cap, another doe-brown laundry girl, with scowling face and downcast eyes?

I remembered the tale of the kitchen princess, and the prince who sought her. And if I'd had a knife with me, instead of an armful of linen sheets, I would have slaughtered them both on the spot, and left their bed awash with blood, her eyes on his pillow, his tongue at her feet, and her cut throat like the widest of smiles—

But I had no knife. Instead I felt a curious numbness. The hawthorn charm would work, I knew. But could it make him see me?

I left the chamber as soon as I could. My heart was caged and beating. I stood outside in the passageway, my back to the wall, and tried to breathe. The hawthorn charm was still in my hand. There would be no chance to use it now. But I did not care. My rage was gone. I wanted to die. I wanted nothing more than to curl up like a dead leaf and blow away.

But now, back in my hut of split logs, my courage has returned to me. I shall write him a letter, and send it by my own means. The white-headed crow will deliver it, and await his answer. Whatever the reason for his change of heart, I shall not accept it without hearing the truth in his own words.

The hawthorn was right: if William is faithless, I should not blame Fiona. Fiona is nothing. She has no power. If she had, she would have seen through my laundry maid's disguise. And if I were to be rid of her, there would be another Fiona. No, I must speak with William, and find my way back to his heart, for I cannot yet believe that he could have forgotten me. And so I write my letter of love, and hope that I can find the words.

My dearest WILLIAM,

If You ever cared for me, Heed me now.

I Know Not why You have abandoned me. I was Your love. You are Mine still. My Heart is true. I cannot Believe that You would change. Please send

me Your Answer by the White-Headed Crow. It
Knows Me. It will Find Me. I implore You, write,
and comfort Me, for My Heart aches, and I can Think
of Nothing else but You.
  My Love for Ever,
  Malmuira

TWO

I waited all day for his answer. The white-headed crow flew off at dawn, but it was almost dusk before I heard its harsh cry overhead. A few minutes later, it landed on a low branch by the firepit. It was carrying a folded piece of paper.

I paid the white-headed crow its fee of honey-cakes and slowly read:

> *Dear Malmuira,*
>
> *I am most sincerely sorry if you feel that I have misled you. But my father has ordered me to make my P-O-S-I-T-I-O-N clear. Whatever my warmer feelings, I cannot allow my P-A-R-T-I-A-L-I-T-Y to blind me to my duty. My rank does not permit me to A-S-S-O-C-I-A-T-E with persons of your kind: so*

wild, so lacking in polish, so brown. Forgive my
B-L-U-N-T-N-E-S-S, and be assured of my contin-
ued R-E-S-P-E-C-T.

Your servant,
William MacCormac

It took me some time to make out the words. It was almost as if he had chosen them on purpose to confuse me. But the meaning is clear. He cannot love me. He and I are too different. I am brown, and rough, and wild. He is a fine nobleman. He cannot love a wild girl. And this is not his decision, but that of his rank, his duty and his father.

I turned the letter over. I had no other paper to use, and besides, the words of his letter were already cut into my heart. There was no danger that I would forget.

I took my quill and wrote these words:

Dear WILLIAM,

Forgive my plain speaking. My folk are blunt. But be easy, and know that I care not for Your Respect. I am not bound by such Duties as Yours. Brown as I am, I love as I please. I would have kept My Promises.

I wish you joy of your Village Girl, and hope to

never see You again. And now that You are free of
Me, so too shall I be free of You.
　　Farewell,
　　Malmuira

I will not cry. I never do. There is a saying among the
Folk: *Give as much pity to a woman weeping as to a goose*
going barefoot. I gave the note back to the white-headed
crow. And then I lay down in the ferns and grass that
grow around my hut, and watched the fragments of
sky through the trees, and wondered how the sun still
shone when my light had gone out for ever.

Three

September is the month in which we put away the summer. Nuts, apples, berries and corn, stored away for the winter. Eat all you can in September, for the lean nights are coming. And yet I cannot eat. I cannot gather hazelnuts and put them away for the winter, or pick mushrooms under the Harvest Moon, or black-berries from the forest path.

Instead, I pick over the stubble fields for the last small grains of the love we once had. The harvest is spoilt: the storehouse shut. I will not see its like again. I pick over every memory, every word he spoke to me. And my heart is a hollow shell, as empty as a beggar's bowl.

I went to see Old Age again, this afternoon in the fairy ring. I counted only fourteen berries on her single living branch. But the hawthorn was in a playful mood, like an old cat, which, from its bed, deigns to play with a ball of wool.

I said: 'I wrote to William. I said I cared nothing for him. And yet I am not free. Why?'

The hawthorn shook her branches. The rags and ribbons and silver spoons placed there by the village girls fluttered, though the day was still.

I told you to give away everything he gave you, said the hawthorn tree. *And yet you wear those pretty beads he gave you at Midsummer's Fair.*

It was true. I'd kept them. The tiger's-eye beads were around my neck. They were all I had left of William; each shining bead a memory. It hurt to take them off, as if I had taken a layer of skin with them, and yet I gave them up without a word, and hung them on the fairy tree.

A gift given freely on Midsummer's Day returns a hundredfold, she said.

I did not understand what she meant and turned to go, feeling heartsick. But the hawthorn tree had not finished with me. Once more I heard her branches, rattling like a handful of bones on a wind that was not there.

They say he has promised her a ring, she said. *A gold ring, for her white hand. And his name, to bind her for ever to his house and to his heart.*

My own heart gave a rattle. 'I care not for his heart,' I said.

Oh, but you do, said the hawthorn tree. *And until you give him up, you will never again be free.*

'But how do I give him up?' I cried. 'He gave me a name. He bound me with his promises. And now I am like a hazelnut that has been eaten away from the inside. I cannot sleep. I cannot eat. There is nothing left of me.'

The hawthorn said: *There is a way. But I don't think you'll like the price.*

'What price?' I said. 'Whatever it is, I'll pay it.'

The hawthorn was silent.

'What can I do? How do I give back a name?'

Once more, the hawthorn was silent.

And finally I realised that she had nothing more to say, and went on my way through the stubble fields, barefoot, until my feet bled with the short, sharp stems of the yellow corn, so tender in the springtime but so like knives at harvest month, so that I left a trail of red behind me on the footpath.

Four

September is the busiest month: with nutting, and storing, and sheaving. This is when the geese grow fat, and the sheep eat their fill on the hillside, and the gnats dance on the silent lake, and the brown bears go a-berrying. But I remain idle. I cannot move. I cannot think of anything but William and Fiona, and the gold ring he promised her, and the hawthorn's words at the Midsummer Fair: *The gold in your eyes is truer by far than the gold he promised you.*

Yes, I was true. What good did that bring me? I was faithful, I was true, and yet another girl will have William's ring, and take his name, and be at his side, and one day bear his children. Fiona, whose name means *White Lady*, and who is good, and virtuous, and will never disgrace him or give him a moment's anxiety.

A September bride is discreet and forthcoming, beloved of all. Fiona is William's beloved now, and she has always been discreet. But my whispers on the wind bring me no news of a wedding. Instead, they bring me rumours of secret meetings in haylofts, weevils in potato crops, troubled skies and storms on the way, but no word of William and Fiona. Could it be that he has changed his mind? But that is a childish hope, I know; and I am not a child. Perhaps I was, five months ago. Now I am as old as Old Age, and colder than ice, and harder than stone.

> *September blowe soft*
> *Till fruite be in loft.*
> *Forgotten month past*
> *Doe now at the last.*

I should be hard at work. Soon it will be Michaelmas, when berries grow hard and bitter. Soon, my folk will start to fly south with the wild geese and the swallows. The travelling folk rarely spend the winter in their own skin. Some will fly south, and some will hide under the dry leaves as hedgehogs, or under the snow as foxes and hares. Some, like the hawthorn, will go into trees, and sleep throughout the winter. But I must prepare, if I want to survive. I have nothing put away.

A POCKETFUL OF CROWS

The others know this. Several times I have found gifts left at my door: two rabbits; a pile of hazelnuts; some mushrooms; the haunch of a slaughtered goat. The travelling folk look after their own, even when they have been cast out.

Sometimes I think it would be easier to die. They will find me in the spring, a pile of rags in the undergrowth. Maybe William will hear of it, and weep for me in the green woods, and know that when I promised him to be faithful unto Death, I was true, though he was not. Maybe Fiona will be with him, his golden ring on her finger—

That decides it. I will not die. I will not give that cowslip girl the satisfaction of knowing me dead. Nor will I be the kitchen princess, with her paltry three wishes. I have no need of a fine dress, or shoes, or a fairy carriage. But vengeance, my sweet William. *That* I can still wish for. And I shall dance barefoot on your grave, and sing like a lark with the joy of it, and soar into the stormy sky, and fill my throat with lightning.

October

The Golden Month

†

One for anger,
Two for mirth
Three for a wedding,
Four for a birth.
Five for rich,
Six for poor,
Seven for a witch:
I can tell you no more.

Magpies: 16th-century
          nursery rhyme

One

October brings the Hunter's Moon, the crows, the brewing of barley. October is the thresher's month, the month of grouse, and geese, and deer. October is the month of sloes, and chestnuts, and acorns, and hips, and haws. October is the golden month, where even the trees are a miser's dream.

An October bride is fair of face, affectionate, but jealous. I wonder if Fiona has her golden ring yet. Word has it she does not: and yet this does not please me. Let her have her golden ring. Let her have her honey.

Last night I went to the fairy tree. There was no moon, and the ancient one was so fast asleep in her hawthorn skin that I almost despaired of rousing her. Around the fairy ring, the stones were nothing more than shadows: some short, some tall, some only hummocks under the turf. The Folk believe that the fairy stones cannot ever be counted. Try it, and the stones will dance, slyly changing positions, so that their number can never be known. The travelling folk, too, have their beliefs concerning the stones of the fairy ring. But this was no night for stories. Tonight, I wanted something more.

I sat by the tree, and waited until the hawthorn stirred from her sleep. Another few weeks, and she will be impossible to waken. I was beginning to wonder if she had already begun her winter's sleep, when I heard a whispering from her boughs.

Why do you trouble me once more? What more can you want of me?

'You know what I want,' I told her. 'I want to be able to travel again. I want to be free of him; of the name he tricked me into accepting.'

A sigh came from the hawthorn tree. *There's only one way to do that*, she said. *And I don't think you have the courage for it.*

'I do have the courage,' I told her. 'I swear it will not fail me.'

The hawthorn gave a kind of shrug, deep inside her hawthorn skin. *I don't think you know what you're asking*, it said.

I promised the hawthorn that yes, I did.

Very well, said the hawthorn. *But the price will be high, both for you, and for him.*

'Whatever it is, I'll pay,' I said.

The hawthorn said nothing, but in the dark, I was sure she was smiling.

TWO

The first is the wool of a black lamb on a spindle of elder wood. The second is a lock of his hair, tied with a piece of red thread. The third is a cantrip of *Hagall: I am the coldest, whitest of grain. Thus do ye reap, and thus do I sow.* The fourth is the blood of a Hunter's Moon; the fifth is the shroud of an April bride. The sixth is the root of a mandrake; the seventh, an adder-stone, carved with his name. Stitch them into a pocket-doll, and place it in the cleft of a hawthorn tree on All Hallows' Eve. As the year turns, the charm will take root: *As ye reap, so shall ye sow.*

But that harvest is for a colder month. October is mellow and deceptive: the golden apples dripping with wasps. The wasps sense the coming of the cold. They are angry, and ready to sting. Now I too, am ready to sting. And I must gather what I need to make the charm before All Hallows' Eve, or find myself unready.

The black lamb is easy. I gather its wool from the spindle of thistle and thorn. The elder tree, too, is compliant: and I make sure to thank the tree with all the correct incantations. The hair is more of a puzzle. I have no such keepsakes from William. But the white-headed crow has the answer once more: she flies up to his window ledge. His hairbrush and comb are by the bed: she plunders both, and returns to me carrying a knot of hair. I know that hair well. I loved it once. Now I braid it into the lambswool, where it gleams October-gold.

Now for the blood, and the mandrake, with pebbles pushed into my ears to dull the sound of its screaming. The adder-stone is taken from a pebble beach thirty miles away, brought to me by an eagle, that cries: *Fool!* as it soars away.

But these things all have a price. The knot of hair and the adder-stone have already cost me dearly. Every scrap, every trinket has gone to pay for the charm's components. And now I must find the most powerful thing – a piece of the shroud of an April bride – which is why I stand here now, with a wooden spade in my hand and a splinter of ice in my heart.

The graveyard lies by the village church. Our people never come here. Nor would I choose to come here now, especially not in my own skin. But without the piece of shroud, my charm will fail. It must be tonight. I creep into the village under cover of darkness. By the light of a waning moon I read the inscriptions on the graves. There are many grave markers here, and the risk of discovery grows with every moment I stay. But, at last, I find what I seek, and my heart leaps in savage joy.

The grave belongs to a village girl, married in April, dead by the end of August. *An April bride is inconstant, not over wise, not over fair.* Married with the cuckoo's call; dead with its passing. Poor April girl. Her name is here, carved onto the wooden marker. It says:

KATE MILLER,
Beloved Wife of SAM and Daughter of ELDER.

Dyed of a Wasting Malady, in the 17th Year of Her Age.

As you are now, so once was I:
As I am now, so you shall be.

But I shall never be as you are. When I have my freedom back, I shall travel into the air. I shall become a thousand seeds of dandelion and fireweed, of ragwort and of thistle, alder and yew. And I shall take root wherever I fall, in your gardens and on your graves. And if you cut me, I shall grow and multiply a thousandfold.

Now I must dig deep and true. I use my hands, and the wooden spade. The earth is stony under the turf. That's good. The hole grows faster.

At last, I reach her coffin. Her coffin is narrow, the lid nailed shut. I prise off the nails, one by one. The shroud is mostly eaten away. But there is more than enough of it left to stitch into a pocket-doll.

I fill in the grave. I stamp down the turf. No one will know that I was here. Poor April girl, unwise and plain. And yet she was beloved. She wore his ring on her finger. I know. I found the ring. I kept it. She had no use for it any more. And a wedding ring is a powerful charm, even more so than an adder-stone, and one that I know how to use.

And now all I need to do is wait for All Hallows' Eve. The year turns: the fires burn, announcing the coming of winter. The ploughman tills the earth: the hay is stored away in the hayloft. And the travelling folk make merry, for it is our time: our covenant.

They call us the Devil's children. But we have no allegiance to your Devil, or your God. We are the travelling folk. We live. And we will live for ever.

Three

Hey-ho, for Hallowe'en
All the witches to be seen.
Some black, some green
Hey-ho, for Hallowe'en.

And now it comes: All Hallows' Eve, though the travelling folk call it by a different name. This is the night when spirits walk: when the Folk set out plates for their vanished ones and offerings for the Faërie. It is the night when fires are lit, and apples roasted in the hearth. It is a time of old gods; lost loves; of mulled ale and strong cider. On All Hallows' Eve, the dead arise, and the travelling folk walk in their skins for the last time before winter.

This is our night. On Hallowe'en, no one questions

our presence. We can come and go as we please among your houses and villages. Even the Folk of the castle will not turn away the travelling folk; not on Hallowe'en, the night when anyone could be anyone: your great-great-grandsire; the Devil himself; the King and Queen of Elfland.

The Folk of the village have built a bonfire in the middle of the green. Straw men, bundles of firewood, and the cast-off clothes of the dead – for the clothes of the dead must be burnt, they say, or face the wrath of the Good Folk. It is a belief that serves me well, for I will need clothes for the winter. I plunder the bonfire. A pair of boots, a coat, a fine wool skirt. Gloves and woollens and knitted socks, as soft as a new lamb's belly. These things I take to my hut in the woods. But tonight I need something different. Tonight, I must be beautiful. Tonight I must have nothing less than the wedding gown of an April bride, taken from a pile of clothes placed there by a grieving widower, and if the husband sees me, he will think his beloved walks, and he will close his shutters tight, and cross himself, and shiver.

The dress is black. An unlucky shade for a bride, perhaps, and yet I know it becomes me. Barefoot I dance around the fire; barefoot around the fairy tree: and in its cleft I bind the charm that I have made from

William's hair, and my blood, and an adder-stone, and I fix it in place with a cantrip:

I am the coldest, the whitest of grain. Thus do ye reap, and thus do I sow.

There comes a voice from behind me, a voice both strange and familiar.

'This time you did not falter,' she says, and I turn to see the hawthorn, standing there in her own skin, all brown and crabbed and smiling. She is wearing my green dress and my scarlet high-heeled shoes, with the tiger's-eye necklace around her throat, and maybe it is the rosy light from the bonfire on the green, but I think she looks younger, brighter, more alive than when I saw her last. The mossy hair is thicker now, streaked with glossy sloe-black bands. Her eyes are sharp and pinned with gold. Her lips, once ashy-pale, are now the colour of wild roses.

'The season suits you, Old Mother,' I say.

'Apples and chestnuts,' the hawthorn replies. 'Cider feeds my withered roots, and brandy makes my blood flow. But *you*' – she glances at my silken gown – 'you are a winter queen tonight. And is that a ring on your finger?'

'I dare say it may be,' I tell her.

'And will you dance under his window,' she says, 'and make him shiver and stare?'

I smile. 'Perhaps I will,' I say. 'For if not tonight, then when?'

She gives a low chuckle. 'I'll walk with you, child. It has been too long since I saw the stars.'

The path to the castle is torchlit tonight, and busy with the travelling folk. The magpie woman; the crow; the stag; the wolf; the eagle. Here's a salmon, with silver hair and a dress of fine-linked chain. Here's an otter, sleek and brown; a beech tree, tall and handsome. All dressed in leather, and silk, and fur, with crowns of antler and of bone. All carrying fiddles, and bells, and flutes, and pipes, and drums, and tambourines.

I join them, and for the first time since I first lay with William, I feel as if I belong here, that I have been forgiven. A linnet in a feather coat raises her sweet voice in song. I join her, and am joined in turn by a wooden drum and a shiver of bells. I start to dance, and they urge me on with stamping feet and clapping hands. And as we approach the castle I see a light at William's window, and a shadow by the curtain, and know that he sees me, and feels the hand of Death upon his shoulder.

Someone passes me a flask of something warm and fragrant. I drink, and dance, and sing some more, until the stars are spinning. And now I feel a surge of love for all the travelling people. The ragged blue tit, the sparrow, the fox, the corncrake and the field mouse. The brown men and women that sleep in your fields, and lurk around your campfires. We may look like beggars by day, but on this night, we are kings and queens, and the world is our kingdom, our playground the night, and the starry night our canopy.

November

The Black Month

†

Marry in blue, lover be true
Marry in pink, no time to think
Marry in grey, live far away
Marry in brown, soon in the ground
Marry in green, not long to be seen
Marry in yellow, ashamed of your fellow
Marry in black, can never go back
Marry in red, wish you were dead
Marry in gold, your bed will be cold
Marry in white, everything's right.

Traditional rhyme

One

Now comes the time of the leafless trees, and the geese heading south for the winter. The last of the apples have been picked; the bare fields have been resown. Jack-in-the-Green has put aside his summer coat, and the Winter King rules over the countryside. And the travelling folk have once more moved on; the fires of All Hallows' Eve burnt down to nothing but embers.

The first of November marks the time when my people go to ground. The fox to his earth; the wolf to his den; the trees to their leafless dreaming. The hawthorn has shed the last of her fruit, and will no longer speak to me. Only the white-headed crow remains to bring me news from the castle.

The wedding is planned for the New Year. Until then, the bride-to-be remains a guest in the castle. The crow sees her occasionally, sitting at her needlework, or looking out of the window towards the distant valley. I see her too, through the golden eye of my stolen wedding ring. A wedding ring is a powerful charm, a window into other worlds. The wedding ring shows me a crow's-eye view, soaring over the valley.

Not that there is much to see. Fog has come down from the hills, and only the tip of the tower stands above the unbroken whiteness. Underneath, it is damp, and still. The forest is nothing but spider's webs. My firepit smokes, and my eyes are red. The boredom is worse than anything.

If I were myself again, I would go into a bear, and sleep until the springtime. Or an apple tree, to awaken with the blossom on my branches. Instead, I must sit in my hut and wait, and know that winter is coming.

I wonder what she is sewing, up in her room in the castle. Bridal linen, I expect, to keep her busy through the snows. I imagine pillowcases and sheets, each one embroidered with her name and his, or maybe a silken coverlet, all sewn with blue forget-me-nots.

I wonder who will make her dress, and of what colour it will be. Yellow, perhaps, to go with her hair, or rosebud-pink, or sky-blue. But no. White is her colour. She must wear white on her wedding day. *Marry in white: everything's right.* If only the poor April girl had made a more fortunate choice.

I have a loom at the back of my hut. Last year, I made a fine brown rug of lambswool and of horsehair. This winter, I shall make a gown; a gown of every colour. My needle is sharp: my eye is keen. I have all winter to make it. And when it is done, and my All Hallows' Eve charm has worked its way into his heart, then I shall dance upon his grave, and be free of him for ever.

Two

I shall start with the dress of the April bride, its modest, blameless panels. A fine dress, for a village girl, but I require something finer. With my knife, I will slash the skirt into shreds of cornsilk, and stitch it all over with rosebuds, and trailing fronds of ivy.

Once more I find myself thinking of the story of the kitchen princess, and her dancing shoes, and her fine silk gown, and her coach and four white horses. What a fool, to waste her gifts on such a paltry princeling. If I had three wishes, I would wish myself into the sky, and fall down in a shower of stars, and dance among the Northlights. If I had three wishes, I would make myself a Christmas pie, with chestnuts and with sugar-plums, and all kinds of sweet delights—

Waarrr! War!

A POCKETFUL OF CROWS

The white-headed crow has taken to pecking at the roof of my hut whenever it wants attention. I draw back the deerskin curtain that keeps the wind from entering. The crow hops in. It is hungry. The honey-cakes are long gone. Soon, there will be nothing to eat but potatoes, and dried berries.

'What news?' I ask the white-headed crow. But I already know what news it brings. My wedding-ring charm showed me the signs of bad news from the castle. It seems the old laird has been taken ill. An inflammation of the lung, following a hunting trip. *A southerly wind and a cloudy sky proclaim a hunting morning.* But the old fool would go by an easterly wind, which always brings wet weather. And now he lies on his deathbed, while his son paces the hallways, and the bride-to-be counts the silver spoons in the kitchens and wonders – *How long?*

If the old man dies, she will be mistress of the honeycomb. And William will be master. At least, until my charm takes hold.

I am the coldest, whitest of grain. Thus do ye reap, and thus do I sow. The answer to the riddle is *Hail*, the bane of every harvest. My seeds have been sown, William. And now let us see what you shall reap . . .

Three

The old man took nine days to die. He held on till St Martin's Day. But by St Catherine's he was laid out, and buried in the churchyard.

Of course, this means the wedding must be postponed until the time of mourning is past. That means twelve months in black ribbons before poor Fiona can wear her white gown. If only the old man had eaten an apple on All Hallows' Eve, as I did – a sovereign cure, they say, against all ailments of the chesty kind. Still, it is too late for him now. I watched through the eye of the wedding ring as the hearse came down the path, the horses' plumes all wet with rain, and William, in his winter coat with the sealskin collar, walking behind, with Fiona by his side.

They laid him, not with the common folk, but in the

MacCormac family vault. His name is freshly carved on the wall of the little chapel of rest. I waited until the folk had gone, and everything was quiet again, and then I went to pay my respects, and to leave a rune-stone by the door so that he would know me. And there, by the light of the new Blood Moon, I promised I would end his line, and see his family home in ruins, and watch his lands all pass to strangers, until they were broken up into strips and even his name was forgotten.

And then I went back to my hut in the woods, and the comfort of my fireside, and my needlework, and the white-headed crow. And when I awoke in the morning, I saw that the first frost had come, touching the grass and the spiders' webs and the ploughed fields and hedges with silver, and I knew that the winter had truly begun, and that my waiting was over.

Four

Clear moon: frost soon, so they say. And the moon has been clear these past five nights, bringing hard earth, a black frost and death to many small animals – voles, blue tits, lizards, frogs – living around the lakeside. The lake, too, is frozen: great flowers of ice blossom around the islands. The ducks slip and slide on the surface. The white-headed crow sleeps close to the hut, too wild as yet to stay inside.

The castle is in mourning. My wedding ring shows me draped mirrors, stopped clocks, and scenes of quiet hysteria. Fiona is not happy that the wedding date has been put back. Nor is she happy that William, still not of age, cannot inherit his father's lands, but must wait until he is twenty-one. Until then, his uncle serves as trustee to his fortune *and* has to give his approval to the impending nuptials. Fiona's silent displeasure is clear. She works on her wedding trousseau with thin lips: saying nothing, eyes downcast. She has had to hire a chaperone, chosen for her plainness.

Meanwhile, the Folk are restless. The death of the laird, so suddenly, has caused grief and anxiety. The old man was popular; his son was raised among the village folk. He swam with their children in the lake; took apples from their orchards. The village folk remember this. Now he is their master.

A death in November means hard times ahead. The winter is only beginning. Over the next three months, there may be more than a dozen casualties. Old folk, mostly, or babes-in-arms too weak to withstand the damp nights. But with the end of the year comes the sense of something darker approaching. Four sheep were taken by wolves last night, and the farmer swears he saw a handprint in the blood on the stone wall of the pen, and knew that this was no common wolf. There are other omens, too. A rune-stone, found in the churchyard. The grave of a young woman, tampered with. These are evil signs indeed, and the Folk are troubled.

Through the eye of my wedding ring, I can see how fear ferments. The Folk are like an anthill riven by a passing cart. The cart moves on, but the ants are at war against anything that comes their way. I must take care. This is not a good sign for such as me. The Folk are fearful and easily roused, and this too often turns to hate. And I cannot simply go into a hare or a goat until this danger is past.

On Sunday, a pedlar came by with a load of baskets. At another time, he might have been welcomed. This time, the Folk sent him on his way with evil glances and muttering. Some boys threw stones. I must take care. Alone in my hut in the forest, I now have more than wolves to fear. And as the nights grow longer, and the wind grows knife-edge cold, I may yet need to deal with the Folk, and to trade for my survival.

Five

More ice, and the lake is frozen hard. But ice in the black month is treacherous, the water still warm from the summer. A pair of village boys, lured by the hope of skating to the islands, fell into the water. One died, the other did not. The lake was not so warm, after all.

In less suspicious times, the Folk would have seen the thing for what it was – an accident. But now, with the slightest thing taken as an omen, the ants are ready to attack anything that stands in their way.

I watched the funeral from afar. The church bell rang its mournful toll. And the ants, in their black coats and winter bonnets, clustered in the churchyard, all encircled with wedding-ring gold. The death of an old man – even a laird – is natural enough, they say.

But a healthy boy of nine, who would have grown strong and handsome . . .

That is more than a tragedy to a community such as this. The mother of the dead boy wails like a cat. His father is bearlike, and angry. The other children, awed into compliance by the presence of Death, stand wide-eyed around the grave. Death has taken one of them. Death could have taken any of them. The fairy tree is hung once more with ribbons and with offerings.

I see them. I take them. A silver spoon; an earthenware pot, a shard of steel, a lace handkerchief. These things can be sold, so long as I take my business further afield. The money will buy me bread, cheese, a flagon of wine for the winter nights. But I must tread carefully. I will travel to the town. There is a monthly market there. I can make it on foot in two days. Two more days to walk back. Two nights of sleeping rough – in a bothy, in a barn – then back to my hut, and safety. And I have other things to sell: charms against the fever, lavender sachets for linen. The townsfolk will buy them, I know that.

Tomorrow I shall set off at first light. No one will see me as I go. No one but the white-headed crow who serves as my protector. She tells me when strangers approach; when my fire throws up too much smoke;

when the wind will bring rain, or the wolves prowl close. She will come with me to the town, to see what lies on the road ahead, to warn me of danger approaching. The white-headed crow is my guardian, most faithful of my people. Alone of them all, she has chosen to stay with me over the winter, to watch over me, to help me survive. And if she sometimes walks as a wolf, and slaughters the sheep in their paddock – what then? If only I had my powers again, would I not do the same?

December

The Month That is Also Black

†

With good ale, good bread and peace at home –
If the snow comes, then let it come.

North Country proverb

One

I begged a ride on a dairyman's cart for the last six miles of the trip, and so, reaching town by nightfall, I was able to spend the night in an inn, high under the eaves in a room that I shared with two other women – one a nun, the other a whore – which boded ill for my night's sleep.

I slept long nevertheless, and awoke to the sound of activity. The white-headed crow was perched on the roof underneath my window and, looking out into the square, I saw the traders and journeymen setting out their carts and their stalls, while the tinkers and gypsies and folk such as I stood by, awaiting their chance of a place.

There were beer sellers, oystermen, butchers and bawds: pie-men selling Fat Boys, and onion pasties, and frumenty pie. There were sellers of wool and sellers of hay, and wine, and seaweed, and leather, and gloves. There were cheese-men, and ragpickers, and shrimpers and spooners, and skinners and all manner of merchants and traders, as well as pipers, fiddlers, cutpurses, thieves, storytellers, pickpockets and other such magpies of the trade.

I looked over my merchandise. Four silver spoons, two earthenware pots, a blanket woven from rabbit fur. Sixty-two sachets of lavender, made from a muslin petticoat stolen from a washing line. Charms against the fever, the plague; a broken heart, a barren womb. All things that I could sell here, starting with the silverware, down the road of the goldbeaters and bronze founders and silversmiths.

The spoons fetched less than they were worth. But the man asked no questions. Thence to the market, where I sold a dozen of the sachets and spells, and told some fortunes and read some palms, so that my purse was growing fat—

There was a woman in front of me, looking at one of the nearby stalls. She was standing half-turned towards me, wearing a bonnet of black silk. Her pale hair was tied in a long braid; I had a chance to observe her face as she looked at the display of fruit. Then she looked up, and saw me—

Fiona has grown fat since I saw her last. Her face is as round as the full moon. She was wearing a shapeless black coat that came down almost to the ground, but even so, I could see her rolling gait, and the way her waist had thickened. The woman beside her, I told myself, must be the chaperone. But now that I saw her more closely, I knew her. A spinster, with a cleft lip, who served as the village midwife—

Fiona recognised me at once. I saw her blue gaze sharpen. She turned her head. She spoke in a voice like a volley of quail breaking cover—

'She's here!'

And then there was William, and everything stopped. The sounds of the market dropped to a hum. Fiona's voice was silent. *Everything* was silent – except for the circle around us both, a circle that was wedding-ring gold, spinning like a wheel of light.

He was wearing a coat of dull yellow wool, with a collar of shaggy, pale fur. His hair was clean and tied back. His eyes were everywhere but on mine.

He took a step forward. 'Malmuira,' he said.

'That's not my name,' I told him.

Fiona, emboldened by his presence, waddled to his side. I said: 'Does your uncle know she's with child?'

He did not have to answer. His eyes told me everything I needed to know. Bad enough that the young laird should have promised marriage at nineteen to a village girl with nothing more than a pretty face as her dowry, but now that she was no longer virtuous, the uncle would never give his consent.

I smiled. 'I wish you joy,' I said. 'But there will be no christening. This child you carry will be as nameless as any one of the travelling folk.'

'What do you mean?' said Fiona.

William's eyes danced here and there, like fleas on a hot griddle.

I laughed. 'I think you know what I mean.'

Fiona said: 'How dare you!'

I laughed again, and told her: 'Even if he married you, you'd be a widow by May Day.'

Her pale face grew paler. 'What do you mean?' she repeated.

I said: '*I am the coldest, whitest of grain. Thus do ye reap, and thus do I sow.*'

'It is a curse,' said Fiona, her blue eyes widening.

William stood there, not looking at me. He looked very young, and I wondered how I could ever have seen him as a man. I'd thought him so much older than I, so much more worldly. But now I saw that he was a boy, fresh-faced, almost beardless.

'What do you say to her, William?' said Fiona querulously. 'The witch, the witch has cursed us! Call for the parson! Call for the nurse! I feel unwell. I may faint, I may *die*—'

'Malmuira, please,' he said. 'No more. You are upsetting Fiona.'

No, I am upsetting you, I thought, and smiled once more to myself. His eyes were on me at last, and I knew that he was wondering how he could ever have thought he loved a girl so brown, a girl so wild, a girl so unlike him in every way. I looked at him through the rags of my hair, all braided through with feathers. I said:

'Cast not a clout until May be out, for on that day, I shall dance on your grave, and soar like a lark above you. On that day, you shall know my name, which is known only to the dead. And on that day, I shall be free, and the sky will ring with my laughter.'

Fiona gave a little scream, and fell into the midwife's arms.

William took a step backwards. 'I'm not afraid of you,' he said, in a voice that was trembling. 'You may have bewitched me once, but now I see you for the common slut you are.'

That made me angry. 'I was a maid. Fourteen years a maid,' I said, 'until I gave myself to you.'

He sneered, sensing my weakness. 'A common slut

143

and a liar, too,' he said. 'An ugly witch who deserves to hang.'

I laughed again, though my heart hurt. So this is what he thinks of me. This is what remains of his love, gone like the knots on the fairy tree, like the first call of the cuckoo. What a fool I was to think that a boy of the Folk could know my heart. The Folk are weak, and fickle, and tame, and they do not deserve our notice.

'Look for me when blackthorn blooms,' I said. 'I shall be thinking of you.'

And then I turned and left them there before they could see the tears in my eyes, and with my pack and my white-headed crow, I left the marketplace and the town, and began my walk home by the high road, so that, when William drove past in his coach, he would not see me crying.

TWO

I spent the night in a bothy, with the white-headed crow as my sentinel. *War, War,* comes her harsh cry, and now that dawn is here, I can see the first sprinkling of snow, high on the tops of the black hills.

It will be good to return to my hut, and the forest, and my firepit. It will be good to sleep all day under the softly settling snow. The sky is heavy and overcast. It is not snowing yet, but it will. The wind is from the north, but when it comes from the east it will bring snow. The wise among the Folk will then cover their strawberries in hay, and take in their swine, and chop their wood, and feed their bees with honey-water and rosemary.

Today is the eve of St Lucy. *Lucy light, Lucy bright: the shortest day and longest night.* In fact, we are still some days away from the shortest day of the winter: and yet this morning feels like dusk although it is still early. The sky is low, and rolls like a drum, and the clouds are like dirty water. I quicken my step, hoping to outpace the snowclouds as they roll, but it is dark by the time I reach the narrow path to the village.

And yet, there is a glow in the sky. Not sunset, nor yet dawn, but a glow like firelight. It comes from the woods, and with it, a scent of woodsmoke, and distant cries of excitement.

A bonfire, for St Lucy's Eve? The forest seems like a strange place for that. Too easy, even on such a day as this, for the fire to spread, and burn the woods. And yet, that is what it looks like: and the fire is already spreading, while men of the Folk, in coats and hoods, move up and down the forest path.

I cannot go into a hare, and watch them from the bracken. But I can move quietly through the woods, and, leaving my pack safely hidden under a black-thorn bush by the lake, I set off to see what is afoot.

I know in my heart what is happening before I reach the path to my hut. The path is narrow, hedged by gorse, but even now I hear them. The Folk are often clumsy, often loud, and tonight, they are armed with torches and wooden staves, their voices raised in anger. I hear them cry – *Witch! Hang the witch!* – and

A POCKETFUL OF CROWS

I draw back into the shadows. No one will see me under the gorse. No one will hear my trapped heart.

And so I watch as my home burns, and listen to their drunken cries – for these are men of the village, made bold by numbers and by pints of ale – and I know who led them to this place. Only two people knew of it. And as the crow calls – *War! War!* – I feel the wind turn, and shift to the east: and with it, I think I can already feel the falling of the first flakes of snow.

Three

Soon it will be Christmas-tide, with mistletoe charms on the fairy tree, and church bells ringing, and carolling, and holly wreaths on the doorstep. Christmas, time of peace and goodwill, and of fat geese roasting on the fire, and chestnuts, crab apples, furmenty; puddings, cakes and sweet wine . . .

Not that I shall see any of this. The rich will give their penny in church, and pay for absolution. *But money is like a great door that shuts inwards on the heart of a man.* The poor will starve this Christmas, as the poor folk always do, and the rich will dine on venison, and sing their songs of redemption, and light their candles against the night, and try not to think of the darkness.

In the castle, Fiona will fret at her wedding embroidery. William will look out at the snow that lies now almost twelve inches deep, and think of me, and of himself, and wonder that I have not been found.

It snowed on the night of my return. Perhaps that is what saved me. They had dogs to hunt me down, but the falling snow had dampened the scent, and by the time they understood that I was gone from the forest, the snow had covered everything, with not even a footprint to show my trail.

They will take this as a sign of witchcraft, of course. Only a witch could disappear without even leaving a footprint. Only a witch could hide away, deceiving even the hunting dogs brought by Master William. But even a travelling girl alone can find a way, if needs must. And, with no other refuge in sight, I made my way across the lake to the largest of the islands.

These islands form a necklace across the dark throat of the lake. There are only two of any size to allow me shelter: the rest are nothing but broken teeth. Only one was still linked to the shore by the ice, and I crawled across on my hands and knees, testing the ice every inch of the way.

Thus I managed to reach the near shore, then climbed up the bank with my pack on my head. No footprints marked my passage. No scent would remain for the dogs to find.

The island was maybe three hundred feet long, a

hundred across. A few dozen trees: some tumbled rocks, a shallow cave at the foot of them. I had some food in my market pack, and my woven blanket against the cold, but even so, without shelter, I knew that I could not survive. I found some bracken and broken trees, and managed to make a rough lean-to against the cave mouth, but it was too damp to light a fire, and besides, the smoke from a bonfire would certainly have betrayed me. I wrapped myself up in the blanket, and pulled the bracken over me, but I slept very little, and fitfully, and when I awoke, some time before dawn, I was aching with the cold.

Most people die an hour before dawn. It is the point of least resistance to the pull of the darkness. An hour before dawn, you can see the pale seam of the night sky starting to unravel: you can hear the birds as they awaken; there is hope. And that is the moment at which they fade, the old ones and the babes-in-arms, the ones that slip gently into the dark and those who struggle till the end. I have struggled for so long, I thought. And now my William wants me dead. And it would be so much easier to go in silence with the dawn, and the snow falling like petals—

And then I heard a low growl from outside the cave mouth. Forcing myself to move, I looked out to see a lean, grey shape facing me with bared teeth.

It was a wolf. A big grey wolf with eyes like jack-o'-lanterns. And behind it, another, as black as coal, with a single pale stripe across its head.

I felt a sudden blaze of fear, and with it, a sting of amusement. Clearly, I was not quite as ready to die as I had thought. I started to struggle to my feet, knowing that a wolf will sometimes pause in the face of a more imposing prey. But I was too weak; I fell to one knee, helpless in the bracken.

The grey wolf gave another growl, but did not attack. Instead, and to my surprise, it pushed its muzzle through the wall of bracken and came to lie down beside me. The black wolf did the same thing, its head resting on my shoulder. And as I felt their warmth begin to bring my frozen body back to life, I understood that these were no wolves of the ordinary kind, but the travelling folk, come to help me.

Who they were in their other life, I did not know. Our people rarely communicate outside, in the open. Some live as I do, in the woods; some herd sheep in the mountains. Some even live among the Folk, keeping their true nature secret: doing as the Folk do; hiding themselves in plain sight. The wolves did not speak, but only lay alongside me in my shelter. I felt their fur against my skin: smelt their not-quite-doglike scent. From time to time, I felt a rough tongue against the nape of my neck; a soft muzzle against my face. Little by little, I felt the cold, and with it that sense of hopelessness, recede. William wants me dead, I thought: that alone should be enough for me to survive. The grey wolf and the black wolf slept, twitching and snuffling in their dreams. And finally, I too went to sleep; and when I awoke, it was snowing.

Four

Snow cherishes the ground, they say, *and anything that be sowed in it.* And so, to survive, I must be like the seeds that sleep under the white-capped earth. By digging, I have expanded the cave, lined it with dry moss and bracken, and thus I have made my shelter as comfortable as such a place can be.

It could be worse, I tell myself. I have clothes, and food, and wine. I still have my knife, and my wedding-ring charm, and my box for striking tinder. Not that I dare light a fire as yet, but this damp weather will not last, and soon I will dig a firepit, and keep it banked and smokeless.

The two wolves come to me every night. Together, we sleep in safety. And under the snow that covers the land, we are hidden, we are warm, and we wait for the hunt to be over. Sometimes my friends bring me meat from their hunt. Rabbit, still warm; and its pelt will help to line and waterproof our den. Or a haunch of mutton, dragged from the hills, or a fish from the river. I cannot cook the meat, of course. But this does not disturb me. I have eaten raw meat before, as a wolf, as a bear, as a vixen. I eat with the wolves. I sleep with the wolves. And though I still cannot travel, I can sometimes forget who I am, and dream that I am one of them, and in dreaming grow stronger.

Five days have passed since they burnt my hut. Does William still hunt me? The dogs have been silent since yesterday. In the snow, the scent has been lost. The ice, too, is melting, from white lace to black. Soon this will be an island once more. And the dogs will not go near the wolves. Their scent covers mine, and keeps away any who wish to harm me.

I try not to think of William. I do not think I believed until now how much he fears and hates me. I think a part of me still hoped that he might somehow change his mind. The white-headed crow said it first – *War!* – and now that she is a white-headed wolf, she says it even more clearly.

I must send her out again. My wedding-ring charm shows me nothing but snow. But I know in my heart that he thinks of me, and shivers, and I smile as I lie in the earth like a corpse, and know that he will lie there soon. This knowledge warms me more than his hearth; more than the taste of blood in my mouth; more than the pounding of my heart. You declared war on me, William: know that I mean to fight to the death. And when you are cold and in the ground, the birds will sing, and the sun will shine, and I shall dance bare-foot on your grave with a crown of may blossom in my hair. But not before you have begged me on your knees for forgiveness, and seen everything you cared for vanish into smoke and ash—

War, says my protector. The sound is almost like a purr.

War.

Five

Christmas Day, and the daylight lengthens to the breadth of a gnat's yawn. From my den, I can hear the bells, and I know that William hears them, too.

My friend in crow's skin tells me that William's uncle has come at last from the city, with much commotion, the result of which is that Fiona has been sent home. The scandal of her pregnancy ensures that there will be no wedding. William's uncle made it clear: the family's honour is at stake. William may bed as many village girls as he likes – he is, after all, the heir, and he has a right to his wild oats – but his bride must be a virgin. The uncle is immovable.

As for Fiona, she keeps to her bed. Her time cannot be far away. And besides, from there she cannot hear the gossips, or see the raised eyebrows, or hear the harsh words. But she will survive, I think. My war is not with her kind.

The snow persists, although the ice has melted into white lace. My firepit is ready now: three feet deep and two feet wide, and the fire burns low and hot in embers, and the pale smoke filters away through the trees. Even so, I find it hard. I do not leave the island. The wolves bring me food from their hunt, and sleep beside me, and give me strength, but I still miss my freedom. My refuge has become a prison, and I suffer as much from boredom as the fear of being hunted and trapped.

But I am not entirely cut off. Three days after I arrived here, I found a boat on the island. It was a little rowing boat of the kind the Folk sometimes use, and it had been moored in a wooded place where it could not be seen from the bank. In it, I found supplies: wine, food, blankets, firewood.

At first I thought I had discovered a fisherman's cache. But when no one came to claim the goods, I realised I must have a friend in the village. One of the travelling people, perhaps, living in secret among the Folk? I feel so alone on my spur of rock with only the wolves for company. The thought that someone might care for me is suddenly, achingly, poignant. To aid me – hunted and outcast – is to risk sharing my fate.

Whoever it is has already done more for me than William did. I realise now how little he cared. But when one has had so little love, even table scraps may serve.

I dare not use the little boat to leave the island – not yet. Too many folk are searching for me – not least, William. And the white-headed crow is too recognisable. Already there is talk of her being my familiar. All I have is my wedding-ring charm to show me what is happening. And so I spend the short, dark days watching the Folk through its gleaming eye, and marking the passage of time against the silvery bark of a nearby tree, and waiting for my wolves to come home, and thinking of my vengeance.

When Christmas-tide comes in like a bride—

What shall it be. I wonder. A sickness, or an accident? Will he have time to understand that I was the cause of his downfall? Will he have time to beg, and pray, or will it be all in an instant? My wedding-ring charm shows me nothing, and I pace and snarl with impatience on my narrow little spur of land, while in the village, the church bells ring peace and goodwill to the righteous.

Six

Speak not ill of the year, they say, *until the year be over.* Someone must have forgotten that. To speak of one's troubles during those days between Christmas and the New Year is to see them multiply like moths, eating up everything in the house.

My spies tell me that Fiona was taken into labour last night. The delivery was painful and strange, and when it came for the child to be born, there was no child, just water, blood and an empty bag of loose skin, as if something had eaten the child away as it lay there in the womb, just as certain predators will suck the meat from a chrysalis.

Of course, the Folk cried witchcraft. Only witchcraft could explain such a thing.

The midwife with the cleft lip blamed Fiona's

appetite for candied figs, for *if figs be eaten out of season, then the Devil will claim his own*. Fiona, in hysterics, denied that the Devil had anything to do with it, and blamed that day at the market, when I had shown her the evil eye.

William says nothing, but I sense his unease. His uncle's continued presence means that he dares not see Fiona. In fact, it is almost amusing to see how quickly he has abandoned her. Her pregnancy was bad enough, but the disappearance of the unborn child is more than he can stomach. Now he keeps to his rooms, and will not come out until the year is done. The time between Christmas and the New Year is a dark, uncertain time: a time when dogs howl, witches fly, and the dead watch the living. Perhaps he feels me watching him, and thinks I am dead. I hope so.

Meanwhile, the Folk are uneasy. The omens have been terrible. Strange births, odd sounds, the unusual behaviour of livestock: everything points to witchcraft. I am, of course, the prime suspect. My unexplained disappearance; my sinister words to Fiona. And there have been sightings, too. An old man coming out of the inn after a hard night's drinking swears he saw me in the sky, riding a broomstick. A second old man contests this, and claims that I was riding a beanpole. Either way, it was witchcraft, and there is a new sighting every day to confirm their suspicions.

From my hideout, I watch and wait. The ice has melted, and I need my boat to go to and from the island. I do not go far. But my friend in the village leaves firewood, bread, cheese and sometimes wine, under a bramble patch by the lake. Every few days, I check the place. So far I have seen no one, not even footprints in the snow.

Who *is* my friend in the village, and why do they risk their life for my sake? To come to my aid is dangerous, and yet, whoever it is keeps coming. I think of Old Age, in her hawthorn tree. Could she be the one, perhaps? I sit under the trees, by my firepit, trying to read the rising smoke. It would be a comfort to catch even a glimpse of a friendly face. But all I see is the island, with its silver birches under the snow, and the darkness of the pine woods, and the ducks by the lakeside.

January

The Cold Month

†

Hats full, caps full,
Bushel, bushel, sacks full.

17th-century proverb

One

Now comes the woodcutting time, and I must keep to
my place on the island. Every day, around the lake,
I hear the Folk cutting firewood. January is the cold
month, the month of frost and omens, and a week's
sunshine in January means the worst of weather in
May. For myself, I welcome the sunshine. The snow
has gone, and during the day I can enjoy the first pale
rays of a new year. At night, it freezes but, thanks to
my wolves, I will always sleep easy. Thanks to the
wood provided by my unknown friend in the village,
my firepit burns day and night, and I can cook my
food again – a fish from the lake, a rabbit, a duck, a
handful of late potatoes. The white-headed crow is
back by day, along with a clatter of magpies.

One's for sorrow, two for mirth;
Three, a wedding, four a birth.
Five for heaven, six for hell –

Of course, I do not believe in such things. Your hell and your Devil mean nothing to me. The Folk are so concerned with sin, and with all the ways to absolve it, that they do not see the way in which the Church has harnessed them. The Church controls their food, their drink; declares when to feast and when to fast; when to have children, when to abstain, chooses when and whom to love. And in exchange, the Church takes their wealth and builds more monuments to its glory. The Church is there at birth, at death, at every important time in between. Like a cuckoo in the nest, it consumes everything it can, and throws out what it cannot use.

The air is cold and clear today. I can hear the church bells. A pretty sound, those bells, and yet they mean nothing but trouble to me – to me and to the rest of my kind. Today, it means a funeral – and with it, another portion of blame for the monster I have become in their eyes. Nothing happens here now without someone invoking my name. Not the name he gave me, no – for that at least, I am grateful. I have become *Mad Moira*, the Winter Queen, the Black Witch of the

Mountains, and in the dark days of the year, the tales about me have grown and grown, like potatoes in the cellar, until there's nothing left of me but shoots, and eyes, and tentacles.

Mad Moira eats children. Now go to sleep, or the Witch of the Mountains will take you. Mad Moira sleeps in a virgin's grave by day, and hunts as a wolf by night. Mad Moira flies on a beanpole, and lines her pockets with shooting stars. Mad Moira's hair is black as coal; her lips are red as heartsblood. Young men, beware; she'll steal your soul, and you'll wander the earth for ever.

The magpies are talkative. They spread the word. *Mad Moira. Mad Moira.* They scatter the news across the sky, across the woods, across the lake, and I feel myself letting go of the past, becoming nameless once again.

Mad Moira flies in a carriage drawn by Devil's Coach-Horse beetles. When the wind blows from the west, Mad Moira is hunting. Mad Moira has a black cat. Its name is Willumskillum . . .

Bad news for black cats in the village. From now on, they will be hunted, their pelts hung on the fairy tree. Rowan berries and red thread are suddenly village currency.

I wonder if William hears those tales. I wonder if he spreads them. Or is it Fiona, who longs to make sense of her little tragedy? Fiona has been churched and cleansed, her lapse of virtue forgiven. Any sin she committed was all the fault of Mad Moira.

Mad Moira, the Witch of the Mountains, devourer of all that is wholesome and good. Mad Moira, whose heart is cold as stone, and leads young men astray with her wiles, and never shows any mercy. Mad Moira, who is as old as the hills, and feeds on the souls of children.

Two

St Hilary: the coldest day, and the Folk will light fires in their orchards, and chop logs against the cold, and wassail their fruit trees, to ensure a good and fruitful harvest.

Wassail the trees, that they may bear
Many a plum, and many a pear.

But it has been such long time since I saw one of either. What would I give now, for a plum, a pear, or even a crab apple? The crabs are all gone from the trees now: there is nothing more to find. The offerings of bread and cheese from my friend in the village provide only an occasional change to the monotony of my diet. And of course I am grateful to my wolves for what they bring me, but I long for something more than rabbit, fish or mutton.

For the first time since I arrived here, I went abroad in the woods today. I left my little boat hidden beneath a pile of brush and bracken, and went softly into the woods in search of the ashes of my life.

By the path, the snowdrops are out, clustering like conspirators. The snowdrops give me hope now, even in the darkest month: they speak of new life, and warm blood, and the distant promise of springtime.

Nothing remains of my cabin now. Only a pile of blackened logs, and the scorched earth around the firepit. My loom is gone, and my weaving, and the wedding dress of the April girl. But I did find my cooking pot, half-buried in the soft ground. I dug it out, and cleaned it. I wonder that it was not taken. But a witch's cooking pot is cursed. Only a fool would have touched it. Who knows what Mad Moira brewed in there – eye of snake, heart of toad, blood of infant? Who knows what incantations she whispered into the rising smoke?

I waited until nightfall before I ventured into the fairy ring. In the village, doors were locked, windows barred against the cold. The moon was young and ringed with white – there would be frost in the morning. I could see the fairy stones standing in the moonlight – some white, some black, like the pieces in a game. The hawthorn tree stood out against the bright sky like a scarecrow. It looked dead, its branches bare, except for its wreath of mistletoe. Even the rags and ribbons hung still, with not a breath to stir them.

I stepped into the fairy ring. My pocket-doll was still in the cleft of the ancient hawthorn tree. Weathered by the frost and snow, it is no longer white but grey, the cloth grown brittle; the stitching torn. When there is nothing left of it, then I will be free again, and run with the deer, and swim with the fish, and blossom with the hawthorn. When there is nothing left of it, then even Mad Moira will be gone, and I will be free of myself, and of him, and of everything human—

I knew you'd be here before long.

The voice was no more than a whisper. Deep in the skin of the hawthorn tree, the old one dreams of springtime.

You thought I was dead. Admit it, she said, and I thought I sensed humour in the voice; a warmth under the frozen bark like the gleam in an old woman's eye.

'Admit it: you thought the same of me,' I said, and the branches shivered with mirth.

Oh, you're a strong one, said Old Age. *I would have known if you were gone.*

I believe her, as I believe that she is my friend

from the village. Only she could have done these things. Only she could have known where I was. *She* brought me the firewood; the food; she brought me the rowing boat. She sent the wolves in midwinter; the white-headed crow to bring me news. She is my friend, even though I stole the offerings from her branches.

'I owe you my life, Old Mother,' I said, and she laughed.

What's a life or two, between friends?

'But what now? What of William? How long before the charm takes hold?'

A shrug, deep under the hawthorn skin. *Patience, child. The seeds are sown.*

If only I had patience. If only I could sleep till spring. If only I were the hawthorn tree, too old to love, too wise to hate.

Run back to your den, little wolf, she said. *Howl at the moon, but silently. And when the Wolf Moon rises, then look to the roads, and listen for horses' hooves on the high-way . . .*

'Why, Old Mother?' I said eagerly. 'What's coming? What do you know?'

But the old tree was asleep again, and would not say another word. And so I waited, and watched the moon, and listened for the sound of horses.

Three

Here comes St Paul's, and the Folk will pray for snow, for *if grass grows green on St Paul's Day, the summer meadows with famine will pay.*

For myself, I watch the hedgehogs, for the hedgehog knows where the wind will blow, and builds its burrow accordingly. Now, she announces winds from the west, which means a month's troubled weather, but I am safe on my island still, with my wolves to keep me warm.

But this is soon to change, I fear. The farmer has lost too many sheep to wolves over the past few weeks, and now he swears he will hunt them down, and kill their cubs, and take their pelts. Once more, I see the villagers with torches in the forest. Once more I hear raised voices and the barking of dogs from the village.

The dogs will not reach the island. But the scent of the wolves excites them. Soon it will bring men to our lair, armed with knives and crossbows.

My friends the wolves know this, of course. I fear for them as well as myself. They must take to the high ground: the snow; the rocky mountains. I have my cave; my firepit. I will survive without them.

In the village, the Folk are at odds. Some believe the power of prayer can free them of their troubles. Some take the opposite view, and claim that Mad Moira is angry with them, and must be placated with offerings. This suits me – or it would, if their gifts were more helpful. But a dish of red berries on a wall, or a scatter of salt on a doorstep is hardly the kind of help I need.

In any case, I am alone again. Only the white-headed crow stays. Every day, she brings me news. Every day, she speaks to me. And now, from the roads, she brings me the sound of horses' hooves against the ground, and I know by the quickening of my heart that the Wolf Moon is rising.

February

The Whirling Month

†

When that six months were overpass'd,
Were gone and overpass'd,
O then my lover, once so bold,
With love was sick at last.

The Child Ballads, 295

One

Now comes the time of ploughing, and the sowing of beans and of oats: St Bridget, and her feast day, and the Wolf Moon rising fair. The wolves have gone over the mountains. I hear them howling from afar. But my friends are still nearby, watching my slow transformation.

The white-headed crow brought news today. William has been taken ill. A chill, perhaps, like his father, although he has not left home this year. His uncle remains to tend to his needs, and to run the castle. Servants left unsupervised are likely to run wild, to steal, to raid the cellars and neglect the livestock and the armoury. Maids grow slovenly, cooks grow fat, and cats sleep by the fireside.

In the village, gossip is rife. Master William's malady

is not the first piece of bad news. *A mild winter brings a fat churchyard*, and this year has not been propitious. The winter's death toll is rising among the old ones of the Folk, and no amount of prayer will help. It is Mad Moira, say the Folk; angry at their disrespect. As spring approaches, the Winter Queen grows angry, bringing storms and snow. She rides at night on her black horse; spinning the dark and ragged clouds on her spindle of lightning.

And so now come the offerings: ribbons and rags tied onto the branches of trees; dishes of bread and salt by their doors. The parson preaches abstinence. The Folk pretend to obey him. But the children play in the fairy ring, and look for witch-stones by the lake, and hunt for goblins in the woods, and tell tales of Mad Moira.

Mad Moira (or *Mad Mary*, or *Mary Mack*, as some of the children now call me) lives in the trunk of a blackthorn tree. She feeds on the blood of the wicked. She wears a thorny crown, and a dress all stitched with black beetles. She watches the world of the Folk, and she can sometimes grant their wishes. To summon her, tie a red ribbon onto the branch of a blackthorn tree, and dance around it widdershins, singing:

A POCKETFUL OF CROWS

Mary Mack, Mary Mack,
All in blood, and all in black
Bring me what my soul doth lack,
Merry mad, mad Mary.

It is a rhyme I have heard more than once as I walk in the forest. Bracken-brown, I walk unseen. Sloe-black, I hide in the shadows.

Mary Mack. Where did that come from? In any case, it is another step away from the name he gave to me. I may have been Malmuira, once. But now Mad Mary takes her place, and I am not Mad Mary. Now I am almost nameless again, and shall be wholly nameless soon; nameless, soulless and free—

Two

February is the whirling month, and this week has been one of turbulence. Harsh winds from the east; rain, sleet, and now the Winter Queen's element, hail, that clatters onto the rooftops and scatters the ducks on the dancing lake.

Two funerals, a mystery illness, and now a growing sickness among the sheep that makes them first aggressive, then unsteady, and finally listless unto death. It must be some kind of witchcraft. Six thus far, and more to come. It could be a disaster.

The cattle, too, are suffering. A rot has afflicted the grain store, and spoilt much of the season's hay. Food is scarce. The grass is cropped away to nothing. The horses feed on bran dust and the pasture is nothing but stones and mud.

William's sickness continues. The doctor has visited twice; once alone, another time with a specialist from the town. Neither agrees on the cause of the illness. The town doctor speaks of an imbalance of the humours, and prescribes a course of leeches. The country doctor believes it to be an affliction of the heart. Perhaps it is. I hope so. I hope he feels some part of what I felt when he abandoned me. In the crook of the hawthorn's branches, the pocket-doll made from the dead girl's shroud is little more than a bunch of rags, stitched together with blackthorn spikes. Perhaps he dreams of me. I think it only fair, after all the hopeless nights I dreamed of him.

Fiona has twice tried to see him, but has been sent away. I think that she is afraid. Her disappointment – the scandal, the failed pregnancy – have made her old before her time. She wears black now, and hides her hair, and speaks of joining a convent.

I have no sympathy for her. She is alive. I owe her nothing more than that. But she has taken to walking the woods, as if in search of something. Yesterday, she tied a rag around the trunk of the blackthorn tree that stands alone by the side of the lake. She left no offerings, sang no rhyme, but all the same, I know what she wants. Today, I let her find me.

We were not far from my ruined hut. My boat was

safely out of sight. I, too, could disappear in a moment if the need arose. Months of living with the wolves have made me even more silent. I move along the forest trail, sometimes on two feet, sometimes four. I hear the wind above my head, the many soft sounds of the leafless trees. It has rained during the night. The ground underfoot is soft and damp. I make no sound in the undergrowth as I travel through the forest.

Over the months of living outside, I have grown even more ragged. Dried mud mats my hair. There are twigs and leaves in my braids. I smell of wolf, and of worse. My clothes are a collection of found and stolen items: an overcoat too large for me: a brown skirt made from a flour sack. A collection of moth-eaten woollens, all stained with blood and dirt and sweat. I look like a wild thing. No, more than that. I look like the demon they believe me to be. I look like Mad Mary.

I met Fiona on the path. I let her come towards me. For a moment she did not see me; I was sitting very still, and I looked like a dead tree stump. Then I stood up, and she saw, and took a step back as if to flee. Then she seemed to change her mind, and looked at me with forget-me-not eyes, and said:

'I knew you were still alive.'

Four months after her miscarriage, Fiona still looks pregnant. Her face is round: her belly, too. Only her eyes seem sunken, older and colder than before. I said:

'He thought he could finish me. He was wrong.'

She gave me a look of hate. 'I'm not afraid of you,' she said. 'You've taken everything I had. What else can you do to me?'

'I took nothing,' I said to her. 'William was faithless. If he had really loved you—'

'I'm talking about my child,' she said. Her voice was low and cold and harsh. Wisps of primrose hair had escaped from the scarf around her head, and blew in the wind like thistledown. 'You took him,' she said, still looking at me. 'You took him with your witchcraft.'

I shook my head. 'I took nothing,' I said. 'My only quarrel is with William.'

'Liar!' she spat. And from her coat she brought out a handful of something like rags. I recognised my pocket-doll.

'You did this,' said Fiona. 'You stole the child from out of my womb. You stole him before I could see his face. You stole him before I could give him a name!'

'I did nothing,' I told her. 'I swear it on my life.'

But I was becoming uneasy. I thought of Old Age. *The price will be high. Whatever it is, I will pay*, I had said. And now I wonder to myself: what bargain have I made with her? And what exactly have I paid?

Three

Another turn of the whirling month, and snow has come once more to the hills. For the present it spares the valley, but the sky remains dark and threatening.

Fiona no longer comes to the woods. She has said all she wanted to say. But sometimes I see her face in dreams, and hear her harsh, accusing voice. It makes me uneasy, even though I know I did not take her child. My business was never with her. It was always with William. And yet, the hawthorn's words – and my own – often return to haunt me. I remember her smile as she came to my door. Her eyes, so bright and gleaming.

How old is she really? I ask myself. From what ancient, far-off earth did she spring? The travelling folk are not born; do not die. We travel; that is all we know.

We have no parents, no children. We fly; we land like thistledown, taking root wherever we can. We grow, we flower, we move on. We are the travelling people.

I try to imagine Fiona's child. If indeed, she *had* a child. A son in William's image, with his bluebell eyes and shining hair. But my curse is on William's line. I said I would see it ended. I swore my oath on his father's grave, and left the rune-stone to seal it. I think of my words, like flung stones in the water of the lake, sending out ripples to the shore. Who else have my words reached? And how much does the hawthorn know?

Last night, I went to her again. February is the Wolf Moon, and last night, it was howling. Rags of cloud across the sky. A wind like a capful of terrors. And the hawthorn, in the midst of it all, black as a nest of spiders, cold as the grave, and sleeping like the armies of the living dead—

Around her, the stones of the fairy ring were grey and black in the dull light. In the village, nothing moved. Only a few windows were lit, the yellow glow of the firelight unbearably remote to my eyes. The hawthorn slept but under her skin I could feel the promise of springtime. Hidden under the bark, there is blood. It dreams. It sings. It hums to itself.

'Old Mother,' I said.

Deep in the bark, a whisper of something that might have been mirth.

'Old Mother, please,' I said. 'Talk to me.'

Once more, that distant laughter. It sounds like a child, deep underground, playing under the fairy ring. I can hear music, voices:

Mary Mack, Mary Mack,
Kept a baby in a sack,
Never gave the baby back,
Merry mad, mad Mary.

Is the hawthorn mocking me? In any case, she does not speak. Only that distant, eerie strain of music comes from under the ground, where the hawthorn's roots, a million deep, reach all the way to Fiddler's Green, and beyond, into Death's kingdom itself.

Four

And now as the whirling month turns again, more news from the castle. William's health does not improve, in spite of an army of doctors. Another specialist has been summoned; an expert in matters of the uncanny, who proclaims that William has been bewitched, and demands all kinds of expensive ingredients for his medicines.

The man is a charlatan, of course. *All* his doctors are charlatans. Through the eye of my wedding-ring charm I have watched them come and go, with potions, and possets and medicine bags, and leeches and chanting, and cupping, and spells. But this man is a *specialist*. He arrived with two cartloads of books, and after a fortnight's study, announced the cause of William's sickness.

William is the victim, he says, of a witch's blood curse. Cast by the light of a blue moon, fed by incantations, the curse can only be broken by rowan berries, red thread, a cantrip of the rune *Raedo* – and the heartsblood of the witch, spilt by the light of a Crow Moon . . .

But there is little chance of that. William has tried to find me, and failed. Now that my charm has taken root, I would be mad to show myself. And yet, I almost want to go. I almost want to see him. So many months have passed, and still I have not forgotten him. I see his face in dreams. I hear his voice. I feel his touch. However much I hate him now, a part of him is inside me. It feels like a splinter under my skin; something sharp, too small to remove. And yet I must be free of him, before I can be myself again.

In the village, there is little talk of anything but witchcraft. The Folk hang red rags over their doors, and go to church, and fast, and pray, and leave offerings under the fairy tree to pacify Mad Mary. It is widely understood that Mad Mary is responsible, both for William's sickness and for the loss of Fiona's child, as well as for many lesser ills: sick sheep; mouldy grain; rats in the henhouse; cows running dry. Small accidents, misfortunes are seen as signs of mischief. Mothers rock their babes to sleep, singing songs of the

Winter Queen. Children make masks from flour sacks and run after each other, screaming. The white-headed crow reports that, in the town, two witches have already been hanged, on the advice of William's man, and others are under suspicion. Beggars, no doubt, or old folk, too addled in their wits to run. But once they have tasted blood, the Folk are difficult to appease. I must take care not to be seen. The rumours fly like magpies. The Wolf Moon wanes, and soon it will be the Moon of the Crow. The magic moon, by which my blood will carry special significance . . .

March

The Mad Month

†

Next did he send from out the town,
O next did send for me;
He sent for me, the brown, brown girl
Who once his wife should be.

O ne'er a bit the doctor-man
His sufferings could relieve;
O never an one but the brown, brown girl
Who could his life reprieve.

The Child Ballads, 295

One

March: the wild, the madcap month; bringing with it the daffodil, the hyacinth, the celandine; the aconite, the violet, the primrose and the crocus. March comes, and the blackthorn breaks into wild white blossom. March comes, with the dancing hare; the skylark's song of freedom. March comes in, and Winter turns, hand in hand with hopeful Spring, as once more the dance of the seasons begins, and the land awakens at their feet.

But the cold is not over yet. Last month was mild, and the villagers fear the snap of a blackthorn winter. The Winter Queen grows ever more cruel as her power fades. But in the fairy ring, Old Age hums with the promise of rebirth, and the sheep grow fat, and the wild ducks fly, and the salmon swim upriver.

My home on the island is once more alive with otters, frogs, and songbirds. In the woods, the birch trees are in sap. I harvest their dark honey. For the first time in months, I feel the warmth of the sun on the back of my neck, and smell the new grass growing. The blackthorn tree by the side of the lake is once more hung with offerings. Some are to the Winter Queen. Some are to Mad Mary. And some are to Maid Marion, or Maia, the Queen of the May, who comes in white blossom and birdsong.

The priest – a town man – is quick to denounce these hateful country customs. There is no Winter Queen, he says, nor yet a Queen of the May. Obediently, the Folk bow their heads, and prepare for their Lenten fasting. They sing their hymns, confess their sins, but in the fairy ring they dance, while the Crow Moon whets her blade and rises like a scythe in the sky.

From the town, the white-headed crow reports several more arrests. Vagrants, not of our people, but sooner or later the Folk may discover one of us by accident. The travelling folk have too often been the victims of their fearfulness; now, in the current climate of fear, we are all of us vulnerable. I of course am especially so. Without my powers, I am trapped in this body, in this place. I must be wary, I tell myself.

And yet the call of Spring is almost irresistible. I

want to run, I want to dance. I want to swim in the ice-cold lake. Most of all, I want to shed this skin, to become one of my people again. But for that, my William must die. This is the price the hawthorn demands. This is the price that I must pay, or be for ever outcast . . .

Two

Today, the white-headed crow brought me news. A letter from the castle; addressed to me, and in William's hand, as neat as a verse on a gravestone.

> *My Dear Malmuira,*
>
> *I know I do not deserve for you to read this Note. I have W-R-O-N-G-E-D you. Forgive me for that, and for Writing to you now. But, for all my pains, my Love, I have not Forgotten you. I cannot Eat, I cannot Sleep, my Heart cannot find Rest, and all for Love of You.*
>
> *I beg You come now to my Side. Release me from this M-A-L-A-D-Y. For the Love you once bore me, I pray, have Pity on my Suffering.*
>
> *Your Ever Devoted,*
> *William*

I read the letter once again, following with my fingertip. Then I waited until dark and headed for the fairy ring.

The hawthorn was sleeping, as always. But I could feel her awakening, slowly, under her jacket of bark. And if I listened carefully, I could still hear laughter, deep beneath the half-frozen ground, and the echo of children's voices.

'Old Mother, can you hear me?'

No answer. Just the wind in the trees.

'He wrote me a letter, Old Mother. He sent it with the white-headed crow. He writes that he still loves me. He says he can't live without me.'

The hawthorn gave a kind of sigh, deep in the folds of her winter skin. *And do you believe him?*

'No,' I said.

And yet, you mean to go to him.

'Is it so very obvious?'

Everything is very obvious when you're as old as I am, she said.

'Of course, he's lying,' I went on. 'This is a trap.'

Of course it is. So, will you go?

'It would be madness to go,' I said. And yet we both knew I would. I knew it, just as the salmon knows to swim upriver; just as the hedgehog knows which way the winter winds are blowing. I will go when the moon is full. When the blackthorn is in bloom. That was the promise I made him, so long ago at the midwinter fair. It would be madness, and yet I must. For have I not a debt to repay? And am I not Mad Mary?

Three

I do not believe him. I am no longer the innocent girl of a year ago. And yet his words still trouble me more than I expected. *I cannot Eat, I cannot Sleep . . . and all for Love of You.* I know it is a lie, and yet my heart will not believe it so. Instead it dances like a star, and leaps like a salmon, and aches like a stone, and there is nothing I can do to still its wild and hopeful song.

This morning, the hawthorn came to me, quite un-expectedly, out on the lake. I almost did not know her: the spring has brought her back to life. Now her hair is as dark as my own; her face, though not young, is fresh and unlined. In my green dress and tiger's-eye beads, she looks like a mother, no longer a crone.

'The season suits you, Mother,' I said.

She smiled. Her eyes were as dark as the lake.

'You gave me something, once,' she said. 'Now I have a gift for you.'

And opening her pack, she brought out something that I recognised. It was my gown, my black silk gown, made from the April girl's wedding dress. All embroidered with roses, and leaves, and tiny silk forget-me-nots.

'I took it when they came looking for you. I thought you might need it again, some day.'

I reached out my hand to touch it: the careful, intricate needlework. It seems so very long ago that I made it. So long ago that I barely recall how it felt to have something so beautiful.

'You're still wearing that wedding ring,' said the hawthorn.

'Yes, I know.'

For a moment I was silent. Then:

'I wanted him to see me,' I said. 'The way he saw Fiona.'

And in that moment, I knew it was true. I would have sacrificed everything I had to be Fiona. To shed my skin, my clothes, myself. To be one of his village girls. Primrose-pretty, cowslip-pale, purring like a pussycat.

But we do not go into the Folk. The Folk have names – the Folk have *souls*. These things are what make us different. These things exist to protect them against such predators as I.

'Take it,' said the hawthorn. 'It's yours. Wear it when you go to him.'

I took the dress, remembering the tale of the kitchen princess. But the hawthorn is no good fairy, helping me to win my prince. And yet she gave me back my dress. Does she *want* me to go to him?

'There's something I need to know,' I said. 'About Fiona's baby.'

The hawthorn shrugged. 'What baby?' she said.

'You took it,' I insisted. 'Why?'

The hawthorn smiled. In that moment, I thought she looked very beautiful. 'You already know why,' she said.

And I did. In my heart I have always known. Because we are the travelling folk. We are not born. We do not die. We are the cuckoo and the hare; the hawthorn and the mistletoe. We have no families, no home. We are the children of everywhere. Our cradle is the open heath. Our bloodline is the oldest of all. And we will not die, or sicken, or fade, but laugh, and dance, and hunt, and soar; and take what we can from the tame ones, the Folk, whose names and souls protect them. We take what we must, and never look back, and scatter our seeds to the four winds, and into the mountains, and over the sea, and all across the starry sky.

Four

March comes in sheep's clothing, as do I. But it will go out with a lion's roar. The white-headed crow keeps me abreast of all news from the castle, but it is not enough. I keep thinking of William's letter, and of the hawthorn's gleaming eyes, and of Fiona's baby.

Fiona has not spoken to me since she sought me out in the woods. In fact, as far as I can see, Fiona has not left her house, not even to go to church. She stays inside, with the curtains drawn, and my wedding-ring charm shows me nothing. Not that I care for Fiona, and yet I think about her often.

I want to tell her the child still lives, safe in the arms of the travelling folk. Nameless, it will always be wild, and fly with the crow and the magpie. Soulless, it will never die, but go into the world again, until the world is ended. This ought to be a comfort to her, if she cares about her child. But the Folk are often strange. Who knows what she thinks? And why do I care?

Soon, the Crow Moon will be full. The hare will dance on the hillside. And maybe it is the March wind, or maybe some darker magic at work, but somehow today I am restless. Nothing can hold my attention: not the song of the blackbird, or the gnats over the lake, or the clouds in the cold blue sky. Today, something larger calls to me.

The road to the castle is safe enough – as long as I travel by night. No one sees me. The fat Crow Moon is not yet risen. My heart beats fast, remembering the last time I travelled by this path, and my bare feet are sore with walking. By the time I arrive, the sky has grown pale. The brown hills are still capped with snow. The path is lined with daffodils. I sit on the ground and watch the dawn that comes up like a primrose, and tell myself that my one true love is watching from his window.

But my one love was not true. I know that in my heart, and yet my heart does not believe me. The hawthorn would tell me that this is why my skills have not returned; that only by his death will I be free. Over the winter, I believed; and yet, with the spring, my mad heart leaps, and once more, I risk everything.

Like the kitchen princess in the tale, I have tried to make myself beautiful. The lake is still as cold as ice, and yet I have washed my hands and face, and combed out the dirt and leaves from my hair. The wedding gown of the April girl is not as suitable for March as my overcoat and scarf, but it is good to feel the silk on my skin. I have no shoes; I have no coach; and yet I can almost imagine what it would be to have him here at my side again; to have him really *see* me—

Time! Time! Overhead, a magpie croaks. Its warning jolts me from my dream. The morning moon is pale in the sky. Soon, the sun will follow. My wedding-ring charm shows me William's room, curtained still against the night.

This is my moment, I tell myself. I shall go to his bedside. I shall walk, and never run. And I shall look into his eyes, and see myself reflected there, and know that his weakness is my strength, his helplessness my power . . .

Five

I came in through the servants' door, as I have done so many times as a housecat or a rat. But this time, I came as my own self, barefoot on the cold stone floor, and, skirting the busy kitchen, with its great ovens, and spits, and fireplace, I found my way upstairs and along the passageway to William's door.

There was no one there. No maid, no manservant, no doctor. It was still early, and I guessed the household was not yet fully awake. In any case, I walk like a ghost. No one saw me enter. The curtains were drawn: the room was dark; but I could see the canopied bed that I had once shared with William, with its coverlet of silk and its curtains of dull gold brocade. I could see the pillows on which my head had lain so close to his; and I could smell the scent of him, so like the scent of the ocean.

'William,' I said.

He stirred. He turned his head towards me. Sleepy in the darkness, his face a blur. And yet there was something not quite right. Something in the way he moved, perhaps. Something in the scent of him, the scent, not of a sick man, nor even of a young one . . .

'Is it really you?' he said. And his voice was not like William's voice, but deeper, and more powerful. And his hand on mine felt different; not at all like a sick man's hand, but like the massive paw of a brown bear awakening from slumber.

The big hand tightened over my wrist. And now I knew that, whoever it was, this man was not William. I could feel his strangeness; smell the tobacco scent of him, and the night sweat, and the rage.

I tried to pull away, and he laughed. He was stronger by far than I. And suddenly I knew who he was – William's doctor, the man of books, who had hanged so many of the Folk in his search for Mad Mary.

He must have changed quarters with William, in the hope that I would come. He must have read his letter to me – maybe even dictated it. And knowing my nature as he did, all he had to do after that was wait for me to take the bait, even though I knew that it was filled with hooks and needles. And he had a knife, of course; because all he needed to break the charm was my heartsblood, spilt under a full Crow Moon.

The man called out in a loud voice: 'I have her, my Lord! Come quickly!'

There came the sound of a muffled reply from the curtained anteroom. Even through the curtain, I recognised my William's voice. Soon, there would be servants, guards, bearing swords and pikestaffs. Soon the curtains would be drawn, revealing the ghost moon in the sky . . .

He pulled me towards him, pinning my arms. There came a sound of tearing silk. The clothes of the dead never last, they say, and the April girl's dress had given way. A stretched seam tore across my breast, and suddenly I was afraid.

The doctor held me close, and laughed. 'What did you think you were doing?' he said. 'Did you think to seduce my Lord in your stolen finery?'

Perhaps I did, I thought. Perhaps I needed to believe. My eyes had seen, my ears had heard; and yet still my heart could not bear the truth. Perhaps it never would, I thought, until it felt the blade go in.

Once more, he laughed. 'You stupid slut. How could you ever believe that he could care for one of your kind?'

I said, though my voice was trembling: 'Sir, my kind are everywhere. They are in the air you breathe, and in the dark under your bed, and when you die, and lie in the grave, my kind will be there to feed on you.'

He laughed and pulled me closer. 'Bold words.'

And now I could smell the musk of him, the wild and hot excitement. There was no fear. No fear at all. Only exhilaration, and the promise of violence.

They think they know me, I told myself. *They think I am one of their village girls. They think I will scream, and struggle, and cry, and let them take from me what they can . . .*

Suddenly, I was no longer afraid. I was not even angry. Does the wolf feel anger when it turns against the hunter? Does the crow feel anger when it feeds upon the carrion? Instead, I felt something inside me swell and surge like an ocean; lash out like a striking snake; scatter like a flight of birds. I fought, and kicked, and clawed, and bit, and then, somehow I was *out of* myself, and hovering serenely over the two thrashing forms on the bed, and someone had torn down the curtain, and sunlight was streaming into the room, and there was blood – oh, so much blood – all over the golden coverlet . . .

Then, like a stone falling into the lake, I was back in my skin again. Something hurt: my dress was torn; there was a heavy weight on my chest. And there was William, by the bed, in his nightshirt, pale as the Crow Moon.

'Oh, my God. What have you done?'

I tried to breathe. It hurt my chest. I struggled against the dead weight of the doctor, lying on top of me. My wedding dress was drenched with blood. My arms were slashed and bleeding. But the doctor was dead, and I pushed him aside, and found the blade was in my hand, grinning like an open throat.

Mary Mack, Mary Mack,
All in blood, and all in black . . .

I started to laugh. It was all too much. The dead man, the Crow Moon, and the way William was staring at me, as if I were Lord Death himself come to take his soul. It was all too terrible, all too absurd for anything but laughter. And the laughter was like a giant wave that swept me into the primrose sky, so that I was thistledown, and fireworks, and starlight.

William had dropped to his knees. I could see him from above. I could see myself, too, but I was unimportant. Poor little brown girl, in her torn dress. I could almost feel sorry for her. Let her go, I told myself. Let her crawl away to die, like a fox caught in a trap. I was free of her at last, and wild, and nameless once again.

'Have pity,' said William. 'I was wrong. I made a mistake. Forgive me.'

Forgive you? I repeated. My voice came both from the brown girl, and from everywhere else, it seemed; from the sky, and from the sheep grazing on the open heath, and from the roots under the ground, and the blossoms all ready to break into life. *You called me ugly, and a slut. You lied and you betrayed me. Worse than that, you named me. And when I was yours, you cast me aside like a faded garland. How can I forgive you?*

'Just let me live,' said William. 'Please, please; I want to be free.'

I blinked, and once more I was the girl, looking out

from the girl's eyes. It hurt, and I felt dizzy, and yet it felt good to see him on his knees in front of me, and to smile, and feel the blood on my arms, and know that I had won at last.

'I'll make you a promise, my love,' I said. And I pulled the golden wedding ring from my bloody finger. 'Take this as token of my goodwill and forgiveness.'

William took the ring, his face contorted with fear and disgust.

I came a little closer. Now I could see myself in his eyes, like a ghost of summertime.

'My vow to you will be as true as any made in church,' I said. 'And any village maiden knows that gold is a binding promise. Wear this for me, until May Eve. Wear it, and think of me every night. Wear it, as your skin grows cold, and your heart beats ever more slowly. And when you are under the ground at last, I will dance for a year and a day, and sing with the voice of a nightingale.'

And with that I fled from the castle, barefoot in my ruined dress, until I reached the lakeside, and finally collapsed there underneath the blackthorn tree, with my warm blood soaking into its roots and my open eyes reflecting the sky.

April

The Hawthorn Month

†

'Prithee,' said he, 'forget, forget,
Prithee forget, forgive;
O grant me yet a little space,
That I may be well and live.'

'O never will I forget, forgive,
So long as I have breath;
I'll dance above your green, green grave
Where you do lie beneath.'

The Child Ballads, 295

One

Today I am the bird of spring, singing cuckoo over the woods. The village Folk hear my song, and smile, and know that winter is over. The Winter Queen is fading, and the May Queen comes to take her place. The children play a skipping game. Only I hear the words they sing:

Cuckoo, cherry tree,
Good bird tell me,
How many years before I die?
One . . . Two . . . Three . . . Four . . .

The children know what their parents do not. They understand things better. They *know* there are witches in the woods, and serpents under the silent lake. They know that if they step on a crack, their mother's life will be forfeit. And they know that the May Queen, for all her youth and beauty, still hungers for their young flesh, and must be appeased with offerings.

I do not know how long I lay underneath the blackthorn tree. When I came to my senses at last, it was night. The stars were out. Above me I could see Corvus, the Crow, and Venus, under her spread wing. I tried to sit up. I was aching with cold. I reeked of blood and sweat – my own, and that of the hateful doctor. My arms were laddered with deep cuts. My dress was nothing but bloody rags. But I was free again, and it felt good to be there under the stars, and to know that my waiting was over.

The white-headed crow was roosting on one of the upper branches. When I began to move, she hopped down, cocking her head attentively. In the starlight, she looked like a toy. She almost seemed to be smiling.

'You again,' I said.

Crawk.

'I did as you said. I am free of him.'

Not quite, said the white-headed crow. *There is one thing left to be done.*

'What now?' I said.

May Eve, said the crow. *Come to me when the Milk*

Moon wanes. When the fairy tree is in bloom. There we shall meet face to face, in our skin, and there we shall celebrate your rebirth.

Then it flew off, and I was left to return to my home on the island. I dressed my wounds with betony, and lamp oil, and a splash of wine. I wrapped myself in blankets and furs, and slept for forty-eight hours, and waking at last in the morning sun, went into an otter in the lake, and hunted, and swam, and played with my cubs, and fed, and sunned myself on the rock, and stayed in the otter's skin for so long that I almost forgot I was a girl, dreaming of being an otter.

Two

Thus I spent the next two weeks; sleeping in my own skin, but travelling elsewhere by day. I was a wild horse on the heath, a skylark over the wild blue hills. I was a green fern, coiled like a snake; a king crow, pecking carrion. Every day I travelled; every evening, I returned. And thus I grew stronger every day; stronger and more certain.

Travelling as a magpie, I heard of the death of the doctor. *Witchcraft*, say the servants. *Mad Mary*, whisper the Folk. In any case, the body was buried in secret, in an unmarked grave, at the back of the village churchyard. In the skin of a tawny owl, I watched them put him in the ground, and when they were gone, I left a pebble inscribed with the rune *Hagall*, along with the head of a black rat, to show my respect for the deceased.

A POCKETFUL OF CROWS

A week ago, I decided to move from the little island. William's men have been here again, with hunting dogs and with crossbows. I still have my boat, and have taken it to the far side of the lake, to a cavern concealed behind a curtain of falling water. The spring rains have swollen the mountain stream, and made the entrance invisible. There is space inside the cave for my boat, my bedding and my possessions. And crossing the water keeps me safe from the dogs that might pick up my scent. Far across the lake, I can hear the sounds of their fruitless searching.

I find them almost ridiculous now. I almost pity their efforts. In the shape of a small brown goat, I taunt the hapless hunters. I steal a pack; I scatter the food; I run off with a pair of boots and set the dogs a-barking. And yet, the game soon tires me. I am too old for such childish things.

And today, I am the first cuckoo of spring, counting out the final days of William MacCormac.

Cuckoo, cherry tree,
Good bird tell me,
How many days before I die?
One . . . Two . . . Three . . .

Three

Meanwhile, news from the castle is that William grows weaker. No one knows what ails him, and the doctors have given up hope. The men he sent to hunt me have all gone back to the castle. Now, his servants travel round to every household in the land, hoping to find someone who can lift the witch's curse on him.

Today, I am a starling. I see them coming from afar. On the path to the village they come, asking to see all the village girls. Young Master William, they say, will marry the girl who can break the spell, and bestow all his fortune upon her; lands, gold and cattle.

The village girls are eager to please. Their parents, even more so. There is a fortune to be had for the lucky one who succeeds. Two or three of the bolder girls step forward, ready to volunteer. The servants escort them respectfully back to the castle, where they are kept safely under guard for William to identify.

Mad Mary can change her appearance, they say. She could be any of these girls. And William is running short of time. Pale, his body racked with pains, he searches for his Malmuira; but I have gone into a hare, into a rat, into a frog, into a weeping willow, and I am nowhere to be found.

I think of the tale of the kitchen princess, and of the prince who loved her. What a fool that princeling was, to seek her by her finery. If William had loved me, then he would have known me anywhere: in a fish, a fox, a goat, a bat, a branch of blackthorn. He would have known and loved me wherever I chose to travel, and he would have wanted to be with me, whatever the cost to his heart or soul. But I no longer care for that. Now I am in everything. Now I am the wind, the rain, the love-knots on the hawthorn tree. Now I am the beetles that will feed on his shroud, come May Day.

Four

The showery month brings light and life: and the hawthorn is ready to break into bloom. I see the buds as they thicken: the leaves closely followed by blossom. It smells of milk and honey. The old Folk pick the hawthorn buds. They call them *Poor Man's Bread and Cheese*, and many a hungry traveller has taken strength from those pale-green shoots.

But no one plunders the fairy tree. She is too old, too brittle. And yet this year she is full of life; laden with blossom; heavy with the nectar of her six-month sleep. Last year she was half-dead but now she is white from head to toe. Now she is bridal; now she is fine. The season has been good to her.

Meanwhile, the Milk Moon sharpens its horns. The white-headed crow now calls to me. *Soon it will be time,* she says, *and everything will be back in its place.*

I have returned to my island, now that the immediate danger is past. I like it better than the cave, which is cold and cheerless. My firepit is lit once more: to avoid being seen, I filter the smoke between a grid of branches. My shelter is intact; the men must not have come to the island. Everything in its place again: everything in order.

And yet something disturbs me. Perhaps it is the church bells that ring so loud on Sundays. Or perhaps it is the Milk Moon, so like that moon a year ago, that watched me as I lay in the grass, and saw Fiona place her charm, and whisper her spell to the May Queen. I did not see her face, and yet it must have been Fiona. It was she who led me to William, that bright and clear May morning; she who made the adder-stone charm that set all this into motion. I wonder what she is doing now. I have not seen her, even once. She stays in her house, the curtains drawn, and will not come out for anyone. I wonder what she does in there. Even as a bird or a cat, I cannot catch a glimpse of her.

But in the absence of certainties, the white-headed crow keeps me company. She does not speak, but stays by my side, or perches on my fishing pole. Sometimes she feeds on the crumbs I leave. Sometimes she brings me small gifts. A piece of shiny stone; a shell; a bead; a scarlet ribbon. Like the villagers, she leaves her offerings by the blackthorn tree on the shore, now all in leaf and summer green, and watches from the branches. And, of course, the children come there to play by the lake, and paddle, and catch sticklebacks. And sometimes maidens come to bathe, and gather knots from the hawthorn trees, and pray to Maid Marion for love, and sing songs of the May Queen.

The very next morning I made her my bride,
Just after the breaking of day;
The bells they did ring, and the birds they did sing,
And I crowned her the Queen of the May.

I want to warn them. Do not believe. The ballad is a beautiful lie. I believed it once, but I have learnt the hard way. *Marry in May, and you'll rue it for aye.* The May Queen is *not* a hawthorn bride, but a vengeful spirit, bathed in blood. And she has many faces: Mad Moira in midwinter, Maid Marion in summertime. The Winter Queen; the Queen of the May. Mary Mack, all in black: and Maia, all in blossom-white. And when she is cruel, we call her mad; and when she is kind, we can almost forget the cruelty of winter. Thus she endures, from year to year, taking what is due to her – your life, your blood, your maidenhead – and

beware those who scorn her, or try to tame her with
their charms, for she will tear out your heart with her
teeth, and hang it on the fairy tree . . .

Five

And now as the Milk Moon waxes and wanes, the white-headed crow grows restless. All day today she has fretted and crawked, and now tonight, as dusk falls, she takes to the treetops at last. Tonight, she knows, I must be alone. Tonight, our circle is almost complete, and soon it will be over.

It has been weeks since I left my lair to walk the woods in my own skin. I can see and hear and sense so much more when I am a traveller. But now I feel the pull of the night: the scent of the hawthorns by the lake, and I want to see it through my own eyes, once more, while I am still myself.

So much has changed since last year. I was a maiden, fourteen years old. Now I am old as the mountains. I was a wild rose, sweet and pale; now I am a Christmas rose, as dark as I am deadly. I have shed tears, and I have shed blood. I have been tame, and I have been wild. And I swear I will never again be tame, or try to be like one of the Folk, or turn away from the ancient ways of the travelling people.

The evening is cool, but clear, and the moon is less than an hour from rising. I bathe in the lake – still winter-cold, but the water is clean and inviting. I dress myself quite slowly, in my gown of rabbit skin and my cloak of feathers. Then, barefoot on the soft green ground, I walk along the forest path, where the first bluebells are starting to show their heads above the carpet of moss. From the village, I can hear the sound of a church bell tolling. It is the Eve of St Mark: a day on which the village girls pray for love.

On St Mark's Eve at twelve o' clock,
The fair maiden will wash her smock,
To find her husband in the dark,
By praying unto good Saint Mark.

Of course, St Mark has nothing to do with find-ing love. But the parson understands that girls need to pray to *someone* – and it may as well be one of his saints, rather than the mad May Queen, who troubles his thoughts and haunts his dreams and makes his old limbs tremble.

The bell has a melancholy sound. It reminds me of something. And then I see the full Milk Moon rising above the treetops, and my heart knows what the tolling means: William is dead at last.

For a moment, I feel sadness. Not for him, but for the love that I bore him once; for my hopes; for his promises; and for the loss of my innocence. I am no longer that bonny brown girl that came to him so wild and sweet. I am so much older now. And though I can value what I have learnt, I feel a pain that is almost regret. Must lessons always be so hard? Must battles be so bloody? And must it always be our kind that keep the wheels in motion? The year, it turns, and turns, and turns. Now it has come full circle. Winter and summer: life and death; the adder-stone and the wedding-ring; all echo that endless coming of age. Who can stop the world turning?

I go into an owl overhead, its wings – *my* wings – so snowy-soft, my voice a cry of defiance. I have won the battle, I know. The bell gives me the victory. And soon I will stand once more between the hawthorn hedge and the fairy ring, and see the stones like raised fists coming out of the mossy ground, and stand with my sisters, and dance, and rejoice, and once more join the circle.

May Eve

†

Now when we did rise from that sweet mossy grove,
In the meadows we wandered away;
And I sat my true love on a primrose bank,
And picked her a handful of May.

Folk song, 18th century

One

And now comes the last day of the month, when witches make their merriment. In the village, the Folk hang pockets of vervain and dill at their windows, and make charms of rowan berries to keep the witches from entering. But they cannot keep me out. If it is my will, I will come.

Tonight I am dressed all in berry-black, the better to walk in the woods unseen. My hair is tied back with a leather strip and braided with crow feathers. As I braid it, I notice that my hair is shot with silver. But the wind is high, the clouds are chalk, and the night is a night for Mad Mary to ride, and for good Folk to look to their prayer books.

I make my way to the fairy ring slowly, very slowly. No one sees me as I go, except for a vixen in the brush.

For a moment I see myself reflected in the vixen's eyes; a tiny figure, dressed in black, no larger than a pinprick. The vixen raises her hackles as I pass, and I notice she is pregnant. I reach the edge of the forest at last. The waning moon is a silver ship, in a sea of broken cloud. The stones of the fairy ring are teeth, as white and sharp as the vixen's.

The hawthorn is already waiting for me. Crowned with may blossom, and in the green gown that I wore when I first fled the castle, she looks so young that without these things I would barely have known her. Ancient as she is, tonight she might be a maiden of fourteen years old. Her hair is unbound, and as black as sloes, and her face is fresh and youthful. She looks at me with dark, dark eyes, and she smiles as I enter the fairy ring.

'Well met, sister,' she tells me.

'Well met, sister. Blessed be.'

'There is one more to come yet,' she says, looking into the darkness. And then something stirs, and a figure walks into the clearing. It is Fiona, in bracken-brown, and carrying a baby.

But it is *not* Fiona. Fiona was a named thing: a corn-silk, milksop village girl. This is a woman of our kind; one of the many-faced travelling folk. Her hair is loose and August-gold, and crowned with scarlet berries.

And the child in her arms is bright-haired, blue-eyed, and laughing like a cuckoo.

'Who are you?' I say.

'I was the white-headed crow,' she says. 'I was the maid Fiona. But that was never who I was. Like you, I am part of something greater.'

I turn to the hawthorn. 'How can this be?'

The hawthorn smiles again. She looks young; younger by far than I am now. 'This is the way of our people,' she says. 'Spring reborn, from Winter's womb. Life, snatched from the arms of Death. This is how we carry on, year after year, life after life. Nameless, unbaptised, we are born. We rule the earth, the seasons. We rule the sky, and the green woods, the oceans and the mountains. The Folk call us by many names. Mary, the mother. Moira, the crone. Marion, the Queen of the May. Some have called us witches, hags. Some call us the Triple Goddess. But we are so much more than that. We are the travelling people. We have travelled since Worlds began. And we will go on for ever, changing our faces throughout the year, taking what we need from the Folk, and giving back what they need from us. Good harvest, rain and warmth and love, and the hope of a new beginning.'

For a moment I let her words hang between us like raindrops. And suddenly I see it all, from the adder-stone charm to the fairy ring, from May to December, from falltime to spring, from innocence to knowledge.

'You planned this from the start,' I say. 'William. His death. The child.'

The hawthorn nods. 'This child of ours,' she says, with a smile at the laughing infant. 'This child will be the Summer King, that the Folk call Jack-in-the-Green. Born of three women, he will reign in fruitfulness and harmony until he becomes the Winter King, keeping the land under snow and ice until Spring returns to challenge him. And then he will fall, as his father did, and the rite will start anew, with Summer's child reborn again, and all of us back in our places.'

The white-headed crow takes my withered hand. 'From the moment I placed the charm,' she says, 'you were part of our circle. Life out of death. Love out of hate. Summer out of Winter. A circle of three, joined in sisterhood. For ever, until the end of the Worlds.'

For a long time, I am silent. But now I understand her words. Maiden, mother, three-in-one. This is how we continue. This is how our lives move on. Not alone, but always linked, as daughters, sisters, mothers. And when my turn comes around again, I will be a maid once more, my innocence reborn like the bloom of love-knots on the hawthorn. Till then I am the Old

One, the keeper of wisdom and mysteries. Girls will come to seek my advice, and to hang their charms on my branches. Children will dance in the circle, and whisper that they saw me move, and look through the stones in the fairy ring, and tell tales of Mad Mary. And all through the summer I shall stay, until my boughs are stripped and bare. And then, through the winter, I shall sleep, cocooned inside my hawthorn skin. I shall sleep, and hope to dream; and dreaming, go into a lark, and sing a song of starlight.

The year it turns, and turns, and turns. Winter to summer, darkness to light, turning the world like wood on a lathe, shaping the months and the seasons. Tomorrow is the first of May. A day for love, and joy, and songs, and garlands for the May Queen. Tomorrow the woods will be dappled with green, and the fiddleheads play by the waterside. The hedges are white, and their scent is honeycomb and asphodel, and the birds, and the gnats, and the butterflies will dance upon the sunlit air. Tonight is May Eve, and the moon is low. My sisters are already waiting. May Eve, and a waning moon.

Time for a witch to go travelling.

†

Acknowledgements

Some stories are planned many years in advance; others appear without warning and demand to be written down. This was one of the latter, delivered by a white-headed crow sometime around Hallowe'en, 2016. No-one expected it – least of all my publishers who nevertheless both embraced it and moved mountains to bring it out in time for my favourite season.

It takes nine Worlds to make a book: and most of the workers behind the scenes never see their names in print. I would therefor like to thank all those who worked so tirelessly to help make this book as good as it could possibly be: my lovely, perceptive editors Gillian Redfearn and Bethan Jones; my copy-editor Liz Hatherell; my terrific publicist, Ben Willis; and wonderful production manager Paul Hussey; plus

Jon Wood, Stevie Finegan, Genn McMenemy, Craig Leyenaar, Mark Stay and all the good folk at Gollancz.

Also, my agent, Peter Robinson and his capable assistant Matthew Marland; Sue Gent for her inspired cover design, and illustrator Bonnie Helen Hawkins, brought to me by chance on the wind of a summer's day, whose vision helped bring my story to life. Thanks, too, to my family, to Kevin and Anouchka; to the booksellers, reps, bloggers, Tubers and tweeters whose enthusiasm helped give this story wings: and of course, to you, the readers, without whom no story would ever be anything more than just words.